A NEW

A Novel

HAUNT FOR MR. BIERCE

DREW BRIDGES

BQB
North Carolina

A New Haunt for Mr. Bierce, a Novel
© 2022 Drew Bridges. All rights reserved.

No part of this book may be reproduced in any form or by any means, electronic, mechanical, digital, photocopying, or recording, except for the inclusion in a review, without permission in writing from the publisher.

While the story is based on a real person, this is a work of fiction. All of the characters, names, incidents, organizations, and dialogue in this novel are either the products of the author's imagination or are used fictitiously.

Published in the United States by BQB Publishing
(an imprint of Boutique of Quality Books Publishing, Inc.)
www.bqbpublishing.com

Printed in the United States of America

978-1-952782-44-2 (p)
978-1-952782-45-9 (e)

Library of Congress Control Number: 2021949461

Book design by Robin Krauss, www.bookformatters.com
Cover design by Rebecca Lown, www.rebeccalowndesign.com
First editor: Caleb Guard
Second editor: Andrea Vande Vorde

PRAISE FOR
A NEW HAUNT FOR MR. BIERCE
AND DREW BRIDGES

"*A New Haunt for Mr. Bierce* is a page turner. As a storyteller, I appreciated the surprising twists and turns, and the satisfying ending. The author creates a unique version of the afterlife featuring competing desires and motivations of spirits, within a tangle of honor and emotion. One choice is between detachment from care about others and the opportunity to do something benevolent."

– Robin Kitson, Professional Storyteller,
Stories from d'Bayou

"Bridges follows Civil War soldier and journalist Ambrose Bierce after his death into an adventure in the afterlife that presents compelling characters and inspirational situations. One key to this adventure is how the spirits of this afterlife interact with the living world and the decisions they must make about these encounters. A most rewarding story, well told."

– E. Gale Buck, author of *Vrenessbith*,
Treasured Adversaries, and *A Quiet Service*

"*A New Haunt for Mr. Bierce* is a compelling and thought provoking story about life, death, and what comes next. The ghost of American author, Ambrose Bierce is looking for a new residence to haunt while searching for answers about his ghostly existence and what it means to move on. Drew Bridges builds a fascinating psychological mystery that any reader can relate to. This novel will appeal strongly to readers who love ghost stories or mysteries and any fans of Ambrose Bierce."

– Vanessa Lafleur, author of *Hope for the Best,*
Tomorrow Will be Better, and *Prepare for the Worst*

"His death more than a century ago apparently hasn't stopped Ambrose Bierce from wishing to produce new literature. Unfortunately, existence as a spirit means he can't do anything. He lacks a human form and all the capabilities thereof. Recent renovations to the house he's been haunting force him to seek a new home. But the late-nineteenth-century Virginia mansion has a fresh tragedy of its own, a widow in mortal danger, and to murderous conmen to contend with. Mercifully for Suzanne Hurd, Bierce isn't the only inhabitant of the afterlife nearby. His best friend, Sid (a Buddhist monk who lived 2,500 years ago) and Kiki, a recent victim of a drunk driver, pool their limited abilities to save her life and avenge her husband Dave's murder. And as he spends more time between worlds, learning from and philosophizing with those who've gone before, Bierce discovers he has one last story to tell.

Bridges, with a background in English and psychiatry, dispenses with the stereotyped portrayals of ghosts as either forlorn lost souls or malevolent pranksters. His spirits are thoughtful beings who subtly develop supernatural gifts to help the living as the story progresses. The plot brings together great people from different eras. Sid is Bridges' tongue-in-cheek nod to Siddhartha, Buddhism's founder, while Bierce comes from the Victorian age and American Civil War. Kiki hails from the present day. Soldier and author Bierce disappeared in Mexico in 1914. Nobody knows exactly how or when he died.

Humorously, Sid says that not even Bierce himself knows how he died. Bridges borrows portions of text directly from several of Bierce's short stories. He italicizes the excerpts and provides attribution in footnotes. Anyone fond of Bierce's work and willing to entertain this as a possible postmortem scenario for him will likely enjoy this novel."

– Heather Brooks, *U.S. Review of Books*

"A New Haunt for Mr. Bierce is a ghost story adventure that is also a fascinating and imaginative reflection on the afterlife. The unlikely cast features Kiki, a young woman new to the spirit world, Ambrose Bierce, who I remember as the 19th century short story writer who penned *An Occurrence at Owl Creek Bridge*, and *Siddhartha*, who is affectionately referred to as 'Sid.' Bridges does a masterful job of utilizing a simple haunted house story as a platform for a provocative exploration of life, death, and beyond. Heavy subjects that are skillfully leavened with humor and heart. I thoroughly enjoyed this story. Highly recommended."

– Len Joy, author of
American Past Time and *Everyone Dies Famous*

CONTENTS

INTRODUCTION

By Ambrose Bierce

I have written very little since my death, a circumstance the reader should not find unusual. Those of us who presently reside in the spirit world appear to have little motivation or capability for the creation of works of art, either literary, visual, or otherwise.

This book was written a century after my earthly death. I gave my blessing for its publication directly to the living author, Drew Bridges, through a process that I acknowledge is somewhat mysterious and, to my knowledge, unprecedented. Perhaps through my willingness to be involved in this controversial endeavor, others may be encouraged to do likewise. By others, I mean writers who have departed the mortal world but who reside in the spirit world and continue to have creative desires.

A word is in order about the use in this book of my previously published material. I enthusiastically support the author's appropriation of certain of my phrases, comments, and narrative descriptions, in whole or in part, that have appeared in my work. Mr. Bridges requested permission to do this in order to enhance the authenticity of my character in the telling of this story. I agree with him that he is not capable of using his own words to fully capture the essence of my personality, and thus truly represent my way of expressing myself. He has done a sufficiently capable job of blending quotations of mine with his own narrative. I take it as a compliment that he believes, as do others, that I am somewhat unique and difficult to mimic.

Each instance of reuse of known material is, of course, documented. Each appropriation of my published writing will be marked with a simple footnote at the end of the paragraph in question and italicized when it is a direct quote. We are, however, aware and in agreement that such footnotes may distract from the narrative action. The reader is asked to ignore this marking for the moment in the service of the telling of the story. In order to appreciate this narrative, it is not necessary to know from what specific work of mine that the words originated. Any reader who wishes to undertake a critical examination of these appropriations will find at the end of this book a documentation of their source.

The author of this work, Mr. Bridges, originally maintained the story that unfolds here first came to him fully formed in a vivid dream that refused to fade from memory upon his awakening and persisted in unique clarity even under the crush of his everyday anchorage. That, of course, is an oversimplified description of our partnership. A full understanding of how we communicated is not necessary.

CHAPTER 1

AMBROSE BIERCE AND THE HAUNTING AGENT

S uzanne Hurd wiped the tears from her eyes as she sat alone at her dining room table. She continued to review two document files open before her. The first presented her house for sale with a local real estate firm, complete with photos of the house. Her attention lingered on two pictures of the house: the ornate, grand staircase leading up to the second floor, and the modern kitchen that replaced the small, cramped one. She smiled as she imagined the look on the faces of potential buyers when they first saw the size of the kitchen and the granite countertops that extended for the length of one wall. She scribbled a note to herself to include an explanation of what walls were removed to open up the space and her choice of the repurposed square Victorian gingerbread columns to replace the weight-bearing walls.

The second set of papers, legal documents that she found complex and confusing, were designed to set in motion the court process that would declare her missing husband officially dead. Holding back tears for the time needed to read the documents that would change her life, but not finished with doubt and uncertainty, she asked herself the same questions. *Is this the right thing to do? Will selling the house help me move on? How can a healthy, loving, astonishingly sane man just disappear from the planet with no trace?* No one had been able to give her answers.

Carson, the real estate broker, tapped softly on the frame of the front door. Suzanne at first considered pretending to not hear and waiting for him to leave. She rose and walked purposefully through the large interior hallway, past the ornate, polished wood china cabinet, glancing briefly at the formal dining room with places still set for two, and welcomed her visitor.

Carson paused respectfully before he accepted her invitation to come in. Smiling with her lips but with sad eyes, she motioned for him to come in. Once inside, in a soft voice more like that of a minister than a salesman, Carson asked simply, "So, are you okay about moving forward with this?"

The tears threatened to return, punching at her heart, but only briefly, and she wiped away a single droplet from her cheek and nodded. They walked together from the front door to the dining room to begin their review of the fundamentals of the offering of sale. They took seats at the table, side by side in tall, carved wooden arm chairs, a large picture window behind them. The wall in front of them displayed oversized husband and wife individual portraits in ornate frames.

Her soft voice in almost a whisper, she motioned to the pictures. "I know I have to get these pictures off the wall for the showing. But it's hard. I don't really have a place for them in my temporary apartment. I guess I'll just stick them in storage for a while. Just seems disrespectful, somehow."

"I'll get one of my staff over to help you, if you want?" Carson offered.

"That would be a big help." Suzanne wiped tears from her eyes and forced a smile.

At the top of the magnificent staircase of this 1883 Victorian house stood a lone female figure, unknown and unseen by Suzanne and Carson. She inhabited a different world, call it the spirit world, and indeed, the living might refer to her as a ghost.

The female spirit's mortal name was Kiki Delahey, only recently deceased at the age of twenty-three due to the misdeed of a drunk driver. She had worked as a real estate agent in a firm that competed with Carson. Upon entering the spirit world, Kiki was surprised and pleased to find this other world needed brokers like her as well.

The proper term in her new world was *haunting agent*. She learned the basics of her new job quickly, including the fact that not all properties are appropriate for habitation by a spirit, and that homes that are haunted are frequently lost through fire, flood, or otherwise. It made sense to Kiki that a displaced spirit could struggle to find an appropriate home when such a loss occurred. Equally as important, she was taught that unplanned encounters between homeless spirits and the living could be clumsy, even unfortunate, until said homelessness was addressed. She felt a sense of pride and purpose that haunting agents served such a valuable function for both worlds. She took her responsibilities seriously and, although she had worked for only two years, believed herself to be a capable agent.

Kiki took note of the fact that she was present in this house to conduct a business similar to that of the two living persons below. She was there to entertain an application from a gentleman, a Mr. Bierce, to reside as a spirit in the house. A feeling of sadness came over her. Suzanne's life was somewhat like her own, interrupted by another untimely death, that of her husband Dave. Despite knowing she was invisible to the two humans below, she felt she was intruding and turned away, moving to another part of the house.

In the master bedroom, she admired the tall, graceful large-paned windows, old enough to show imperfections in the original glass panes. She turned to stand before an eight-by-four-foot framed mirror and was startled by her own reflection. She saw that she appeared much as she did immediately before her death. On her way to a business meeting, she had been dressed in her professional best no-nonsense gray pantsuit and adorned with modest jewelry. Reaching up to brush back a strand of her short brown hair, she was again reminded of the limits of her current form: her hair did not move.

She continued to observe herself in the mirror, remembering that she had once seen a movie where spirits did not show any form at all in mirrors. She reflected on the fact that although she still looked the same, thin and fit, maybe even pretty, in this spirit world her body had no actual physical capabilities. Her hands could not lift or move things and she had no need for food. Breathing air in and out was unnecessary. Her feet did not actually touch ground, but somehow she moved through space.

She was again startled, this time by the arrival in the mirror of another spirit, a man. She turned around and confirmed that the man was indeed present in the room. She wondered if his long coat was not once part of an old military uniform, altered for more general wear. His boots were consistent with what a soldier might wear, but his pants were more elaborately tailored. A white shirt with modest trim and impressive cuffs added style with a hint of formality.

"Oh, are you Mr. Bierce?" she asked.

"Indeed. I am Ambrose Bierce. I assume you are the agent to which I am making my plea?"

Kiki began her interview of the applicant for this home with an outstretched hand. The man spirit, unlike Kiki, had lived in this dimension for many years and knew that spirits did not shake hands. In this form beyond the mortal, they did not actually have hands in the human sense, despite the appearance of it. He gave her a knowing smile and she quickly corrected herself.

"Oh . . , I'm sorry . . . I knew that . . . but it's good to meet you."

"And I am most pleased to meet you, young lady."

Regaining her business focus, Kiki continued. "So, I believe your name is Bierce, Mr. Ambrose Bierce? Shall I tell you about the house, and why it has all the elements appropriate for a haunting? Or should we talk about you first?"

"Indeed, do go on, young lady, I appreciate it is a marvelous house to the eye, but having just arrived at this location a few moments ago, I know precious little of the history of it." He spoke in a formal manner, appropriate to his garments that Kiki recognized correctly as coming from a previous century.

Kiki delivered her sales pitch with poise and energy. "Not only is the house a classic build, the outside virtually unaltered from the late 1800s, but the inside has undergone extensive electrical and plumbing upgrades and some structural improvements. The floors have been leveled where it is structurally safe to do so, yet some slant is characteristic of houses this old. It is currently well maintained, and more importantly for you, it has the requisite history of a horrific death and keeps an undiscovered and ominous secret."

Ambrose lifted an eyebrow. "Well, I dare say you give a well-crafted pitch here. In time I would like to know the details of the crime and the secret. Are you a woman of letters?"

"A woman of letters?" It took her a moment to decipher his terminology. He had asked if she had a background in literature.

"Not really, but my college major was communications," she answered.

Ambrose's face showed puzzlement as he replied. "While I am not familiar with the exact use of that term, I think I understand the gist of it. I have kept my mind open to learning things beyond what I gleaned as a breathing being. But now I suppose you are going to ask me some questions about my appropriateness to be an inhabitant of this residence." He clasped his hands behind his back, stood tall and straight with his face turned slightly upward, waiting for her to question him.

"Yes . . . uh, I do have some information already. You were a soldier, and later a writer, both fiction and some, uh, history or newspaper work. Late nineteenth century, early twentieth, I'm told. But I'm sorry, I can't really say I have heard of you or read anything you wrote. But that's on me, not you. I wasn't big in history or English lit back in my school days. I liked business and computers."

"Computers," he said blandly, his intonation not clearly indicating whether his comment posed a question or carried some other connotation.

She resumed. "There are only a few things I need to know about you. First, where were you haunting before and what was the general style of your presence there? Was this some place you were personally attached to, and did you make yourself known to those who lived there, either directly or indirectly?" Kiki presented her questions with an enthusiastic, cheerful style.

He moved away from her and looked out the bedroom window as he spoke wearily.

"I'm afraid you will find my story less than notable. Although I have taken residence in three separate dwellings since leaving the living, one in San Francisco, the others in New Orleans, I have been very discrete, seldom making myself known, and I dare say almost never making myself troublesome or frightening. None of the places I stayed held a personal connection, but all had, as you have said, either the requisite dark story or the terrible secret."

"So why did you leave?"

"If I were one to laugh, I would bellow out a guffaw that would startle and make you step back. That is, if I did laugh. Because each of the places from which I was displaced came about through the most inane and trivial of circumstances. I think the proper modern term would be 'urban renewal,' or perhaps some other term that implies economic progress."

"So, they tore them down for new development?"

Ambrose paced slowly in a circle around Kiki. "Oh, but why could those noble structures not have burned in a tragic fire, or met their end devastated by flood or earthquake, even war? At least their destruction would have been a fitting end. But a parking lot? A 'Walmart Superstore'? How does one haunt a parking lot? And I will not reside in a giant warehouse for affordable merchandise."

"Okay. I see. So, why are you attracted to this place? Will you be bringing a personal grudge or need for revenge? The desire to rescue someone? Anything having to do with this house?"

Ambrose turned back toward her and answered with a tone that she thought showed frustration. "Decidedly not. Decidedly none of those 'ghostie' chain-rattling and moaning occurrences. I desire simply a place filled with some energy that connects to this spirit realm. A place to watch the living world and be entertained. I confess that I do have an interest in this part of southern Virginia because of all the history. If you were fully informed about my experiences you might understand that I am drawn to the southern battlefields of that American war. I have traveled frequently to the battlefield at Gettysburg, and a residence here will provide me with a sense of personal satisfaction."

Kiki smiled and started to speak, but Ambrose lifted his hand to stop her. "And there is one more thing. The name of the house."

"The name of the house? I didn't know the house had a name! How could I have missed that?"

Ambrose motioned for her to follow him down the hallway where a large window allowed a clear view of the grounds at the back of the house. "Look towards the two large Magnolia trees, just to the left of the small acclivity toward the right. I think you can see a large stone pillar between the trees. Do you see it?"

"Yes. Is there something written on it?

"It is a rather old construction. Carved and easily visible on a section of polished granite is the designation, 'The Stables at Old Robin'. I surmise that the larger grounds featured a horse stable and perhaps other farming endeavors, although scarce evidence of that remains."

"I am truly embarrassed that I didn't do my research on this property," Kiki said. "I'm usually better than that. I'll get to work on it and find out where the name came from."

"I believe I can be of some assistance about the name. Old Robin was the name of Abraham Lincoln's favorite horse. I am told that Old Robin walked with the slain president in his funeral procession, although I was not in attendance so I cannot attest personally to that."

Kiki responded with a broad smile. "Sure. You know, I think you will be a good fit here in this house. I believe Old Robin will be in good hands with your presence. And with that, we might be finished here. I don't really have any other questions. Except . . . no . . . that's not really a question for you." Kiki's smile faded.

"What is it, young lady?" Ambrose stepped forward. "What is on your mind other than questions about me?"

Before answering him, she looked down and gave what passed for a sigh given the limitations of absent mortal physiology. "Well . . . you see . . . I haven't really been here that long, and I'm just trying to figure all this out. I'm trying to better understand where I am and what to do with myself, and you seem to have been here a long time—"

"What did you think death would be like?"

She gestured with lifted arms and eyes opened widely. "I was twenty-three years old! I never thought about death. I mean, I went to church and I guess I believed in Heaven and Hell, but to say I really ever thought about it—"

Ambrose interrupted before she finished her reply, "What religion did you embrace?"

"Methodist."

"Pity. Too bad you weren't Catholic. Then we could talk about purgatory."

"I know about that. Are we in purgatory?"

Ambrose paused before answering and gave his response with a brief shrug of his shoulders. "Not really. None of the religions I knew of really had it right. Not even the Buddhists. But one thing that is clear is that we exist here in a kind of middle place. Everyone comes here for at least a short period of time before they move on to what is next, to what I think might be the final resting place for the spirit, or the soul, or whatever name you attribute to what we are now or what, perhaps, we are becoming."

Kiki's response came quickly and enthusiastically. "But I haven't met a lot of people yet and I haven't met anyone who seems to have been here as long as you. And there just aren't a lot of people—uh . . . spirits, around. With all the people who ever lived before and died, it seems like it would be more crowded here. So, this other place, the place you say that people move on to, it seems like most people move on pretty quickly to . . . where? Or what?"

He replied, "There are some things I know and some things I don't know. But I would very much like to make an arrangement with you. In return for you telling me about the terrible death and the grand secret held within this temporal structure, I will tell you what I think I know about this world, your new world. But let me caution you, this information is not the sort of thing that one can simply blurt out. It will take some time to present it in a believable manner. Shall we finish our practical business here? And if I am granted your permission to reside here, will you come back tomorrow and we shall begin our further conversations?"

"Deal!" she replied. "But one more quick question. Why have you stayed here so long? Why haven't *you* moved on to wherever and whatever this next thing is?"

"That is another thing I cannot explain in a simple statement or two," he said. For the first time, Kiki heard enthusiasm in his speech. He reminded her of a favorite high school teacher who could light up a room with energy. "But mostly it concerns things that give me pleasure and things that hold my curiosity. Yes, there is pleasure here, even absent corporeal sensations. And there are also some things I do not yet know, but want to know, about this realm. There are mysteries here, but our conversation must wait. I have other matters to which I must attend at the moment. Shall we talk tomorrow? Meet right here?

Perhaps at the same arbitrary designation that the mortals label as time?"

Kiki motioned to a tall grandfather clock that stood in the hall just outside the bedroom. "The way time works here is another thing that puzzles me, but if we can go by the big clock here, it's a deal."

Ambrose held up his hand, indicating that their business was not complete. "About this terrible death and secret you mentioned. If you are to tell me that it is entirely about the living woman downstairs and whatever misfortune she has endured, then we may have some additional things to discover. I sense a sadness—no, a pain and suffering, in this house that is very old. Far older than your time upon the living earth and the remainder spent here."

Kiki responded with wide eyes and a big smile. "How interesting! And like you, there are some things I know and some I don't. But it's one of the jobs of a haunting agent to find things out. So, I'll get busy."

Kiki said goodbye to Ambrose but remained in the house. She descended the grand staircase, moving past Suzanne who sat alone at the dining room table, head down, sadness covering her face. Kiki left by the kitchen back door that opened to a path leading to the engraved stone pillar.

CHAPTER 2

THE TOMORROW AFTER YESTERDAY

Two punctual spirits met in the master bedroom of the house the next day, as measured by the calendar and clock of living humans, eager to hear what the other had to share. They paused to hear the deep-toned chime of the grandfather clock echo through the hallway. Kiki suggested they tour the house as she began a description of how Suzanne's husband, Dave, had died. She emphasized that the manner of his death and surrounding events and circumstances made the house appropriate for haunting. As they talked, they moved through the halls, Kiki's narrative about Dave interrupted by comments of appreciation for features of the house.

At one point Kiki said, "You know, talking about people dying, especially in such a violent way, would usually upset me. I'd feel kind of sick, but talking about it now, it's just kind of ... well ... nothing. Maybe just 'oh, well that happened'."

"Yes. That is something you will discover about yourself now, in this world," said Ambrose. "The character, the nature of your emotional reactions here are greatly changed. If it is a mystery, it is an easily explained one. You ought to consider it a matter of knowing that whatever identity you once held is different now."

Kiki initially turned away, shaking her head, and then she turned back, gesturing with arms open wide. "Okay, well, I'm not sure I understood exactly what all that means. You sure can talk, Mr. Bierce. But if you're trying to say I'm just different now, well, I think what you are saying is kind of nice. I used to take these pills for panic spells, and worry about every little thing. I mean, I could work up a worry about little things or big things that nobody could do anything about. But I can't imagine getting panicky now. It's a relief."

Ambrose wore a wry smile on his face. "Yes," he said with solemn, faux drama. "Dead people do not experience panic spells."

Kiki continued, "Anyway. Back to Suzanne and her husband. As I said, these two men, after taking the money from the drugs they sold, and then running away from who they were supposed to give it to, came to this house thinking no one was home and that they could just hide it in the attic. Come back for it later. But Dave Hurd was home and when they came in on him and surprised him—and it surprised them too—their whole plan changed."

"So, why did they pick this house?" Ambrose gestured with open palms as they entered a large renovated bathroom near the master bedroom.

"Randomly, you might say, but also looking for an upper-class house that no one would think of as a drug house. You can see it's on a big lot and is well maintained, so obviously the people who lived here had money. Plus, all the trees and stuff kind of hide it unless you're right here in front of it. They thought they could find a place to stash the money in the attic and come back and get it when it was safe."

Ambrose moved around the bathroom, examining the newly laid tile, rain shower, and other luxurious fixtures of the bath. "Indeed. The people who built this obviously spent a great deal of money on it. But tell me, when the old bath was ripped out, did the house scream?"

Kiki was truly puzzled by Ambrose's question. She remained silent until she finally managed to say, "That's funny, I think. Did you mean it to be funny? Was it a joke?"

Ambrose said softly, without emotion, "I am not known for telling jokes." He moved back to the question of the men and the money. "And what did they expect the . . . ahem . . . legitimate owners of the money to do while they waited?"

"Well, as far as I can tell, they didn't have that really figured out. I don't think these two men were very smart. Maybe they were kind of mean-smart, but not wise-smart. But their plan, as I understand it, is that they would just hide and hope the people who were looking for them would just forget about them. They've been hiding somewhere, I'm not sure where, for more than a year now."

Ambrose raised an eyebrow. "So . . . tell me how you know all of this."

Kiki felt immediately stumped by the question. Someone had told her, she was sure, yet she had no memory of anyone explaining it to her, spirits living or dead. As clearly and as certainly as if she had been the witness, she knew.

"It's a story in my head. I know it. I can't explain how I know. I remember knowing it when I first came here. Maybe the house told me. Maybe if houses can scream, they can tell stories." Kiki winked at Ambrose. He allowed himself a brief chuckle.

"How did they kill him?" asked Ambrose, allowing her for the moment to move away from the troublesome question of how she learned the story.

Kiki paused and looked out the small window in the bath.

"They took him with them after they hid the money. They drove out into the countryside and cut him with a knife until he bled to death. One of the men took the lead and the other seemed kind of sick about it, but he went along and didn't do anything to stop it. They buried him in a field with lots of small trees and bushes. It's going to be hard for anybody to find. It's been a year already and no one has found him. The trees and stuff on the land are growing fast and it will soon cover up all the evidence that somebody was buried there."

"And you saw it all?"

"I didn't actually see it, or I don't really know how I saw it. But it's like a movie in my brain. I don't remember following them there. But I can just see it real clear." She looked to Ambrose expectantly, hoping he could shed light on what she was struggling with.

Ambrose lifted his gaze and motioned with open hands. "It is quite a remarkable phenomenon, how we know things, how some of us, you, or me, come to know things and others do not. I know things that I am certain that no one has ever actually told me, but I knew nothing of what you just told me. The best I can do to describe this phenomenon is that information seems to be carried in the air, on the wind, and just comes to you—"

"What about you?" she said abruptly, now that she'd seen the limitation of his knowledge. You were going to tell me what you know about people coming in and out of this life . . . uh . . . world."

Under the man's mustache was a satisfied smile. "Indeed I did and indeed I will. But one last question about all of this: Where is the money, the drug money, the cause of all this trouble?"

Kiki responded with impatience. "In the attic, behind some drywall. All of the construction up there is pretty rough. It's been rebuilt several times, but never finished as a living space. So, no one would notice anything unusual about the spot near the chimney where they pulled off a section of drywall then pushed it back. I can show you."

Ambrose waved his hand to refuse inspection of the money site, then moved out into the hallway along the balcony. He motioned for Kiki to follow him. From there they had a clear line of sight into the great room below. Through the large windows reaching up two stories at the front of the house they could see cars moving along the road beyond the driveway. The area was otherwise a quiet landscape. Below them Suzanne sat in her living room, staring past a newspaper open in front of her but clearly not reading it.

Ambrose motioned toward Suzanne. "Observe the living, breathing woman on the couch. She is filled with fears, hopes, still has some dreams, and on balance is in a hurry to get there, or at least move beyond her current circumstance. Do you feel sorry for her?"

Kiki paused, then began her reply slowly, haltingly, "I think I do. Or, I think I should feel sorry for her. But like I said before, I don't seem to look at anything anymore with a lot of emotion. I think about the two men coming back and what they might do to her, and that would be bad, but I think I could watch something awful and . . . I don't know . . . maybe just stand there and look at it. That's weird to say, but in some ways I don't really care."

"Your representation of your feelings is a worthy account of the nature of residing in this state of existence. I think perhaps this realm is a common destination in order to attain a measure of respite from the world from which we so inevitably did depart. Perhaps the reason for such a way station is to calm and gather ourselves . . . before we move on to the next."

Pausing for her own eternal millisecond, as if lost in thought, perhaps reviewing her life, Kiki moved to position herself in front of him and asked, "So what about you, Mr. Ambrose Bierce? Why have you stayed so long? Why have you not moved on? I think the best way for me to learn about this world might be to learn more about you."

"We will get there, young lady, but let us talk as we continue our tour of my proposed new home."

Feeling frustrated with Ambrose's lack of answers, but happy to return to her task as haunting agent, she led him down the stairs, passing unseen by Suzanne, into the renovated kitchen. "So, here is the grand selling point for the sale of this house. *Voila!*" She gestured with outstretched arms.

Ambrose gasped. "Oh my God! What a travesty! Now I know this house has been screaming with the abuse it has endured."

Kiki was bewildered by his reaction. "So, you're really serious about the house screaming?" she mumbled in reply.

Ambrose responded with a hint of sadness and anger in his voice. "Living humans have no idea the damage they do when they rip the hearts out of these grand old structures. I first saw this in San Francisco. Elegant 1800s mansion, in the Haight-Ashbury, probably ten thousand square feet. They chopped it up for seven or so apartments. The house suffered greatly. I had to leave. The living heard nothing, of course."

"I'm learning so much," Kiki replied humbly, then changed her tone to a confrontational one. "I'm learning so much but none of it is about you. When does that happen?"

"Do not be so impatient. We have many mysteries here. The one we are ignoring is the death of a man and what may happen to his living wife. You say the money is still in the attic?"

"Yes, the money is still in the attic. But you're not giving me much about you. I think you are not seeing how important that is to me. I'm working on this haunting agent job but I'm truly lost about everything else. Who else do I go to?"

Ambrose turned to face her directly, and Kiki felt for the first time that Ambrose actually looked at her, perhaps conveying some real interest in her as a person, or actually a spirit. "So, you want to know about me. Have you ever heard of the Civil War battle of Shiloh?"

"Yes. No. Uh . . . I'm not sure. What about it?"

He turned away from her, then back to face her and spoke softly. "Go wherever you can to find out about Shiloh, and after you know about that, we can talk more. We can talk about me. I will continue my tour alone. I will see what other horrors this house has endured."

Left standing alone, save for Suzanne in the room below, Kiki realized her detachment from care was not complete. She felt angry and frustrated by her interaction with Ambrose, perhaps as a child might feel in the presence of a dismissive parent, with no confidence in the power to address, let alone challenge, perceived hurts.

CHAPTER 3

KIKI DOES HER HOMEWORK

A few days after her last meeting with Ambrose, as measured by the human-designed mechanical instrument known as the clock, Kiki returned to the house to find Ambrose. The musical chimes of the grandfather clock called her upstairs where they had previously met. Unable to find him, she explored other rooms. She found him downstairs in the large library.

Ambrose turned to greet her with an outburst of enthusiasm she had not yet seen. "Look at this library! Until I found it, I was beginning to doubt my choice to reside here. More importantly, I think this may be the reason I have heard no cries or mourning from the house due to those—what did you call them—upgrades? Here in this grand room we have character and substance preserved."

Kiki smiled and responded with what she hoped would be accepted as a playful rebuke. "Those upgrades, or renovations, are the reason this house will have living humans who will buy it."

Ambrose returned her comment with a somewhat more biting reply. "Whatever one calls them, I consider them to be in the category of war wounds."

Their conversation was cut short by Suzanne entering the library. She appeared to be headed to a bookshelf at the back of the room. Her path took her directly into the space inhabited by Ambrose's spirit. He stepped aside to let her pass; she retrieved a book and left the room.

Kiki angled her head and squinted. "Did you really need to step aside? I mean, I think I've seen people walk right through spirits without there being a problem."

"Quite right," said Ambrose, "Yet I do always move aside. Allowing a living body to appear to inhabit the same space as my current form has always seemed a small measure unsettling. If I may introject some levity, it has always struck me as a bit 'spooky'." Ambrose lifted and wiggled his hands and made a face with wide eyes and puckered lips.

"That's funny," Kiki responded without laughing, "But I know all about your humor, Mr. Bierce. I went to the library last night when all the living people were gone. I read in your rather famous book of definitions. Very clever."

Ambrose smiled. "Thank you. But before we go on, allow me to trouble you with another question. Exactly how did you open the pages of the books there to be able to read my work?"

Kiki smiled back. "I was going to get to that. But I'm sure it's something you know about. Libraries seem to be an exception to the rule that we can't move things around, or rather, the books just seem to open up to spirits."

"Mostly right, but tell me this: Did you encounter any other spirits there?"

Kiki's eyes widened. "Now that's something I wondered about! I didn't actually see anybody else, but I had the feeling I wasn't alone."

"Libraries are graced with a great many spirits. Museums as well. I have wondered if some have learned to serve the curiosity of other spirits. Sort of a 'ghost librarian,' if you might grant me a chuckle for that idea?"

Kiki responded quickly. "So, we happen to be in a library right now. Does that mean there is a spirit here?"

A look of surprise came over Ambrose's face. "Well, who is

clever now? I confess that in my pleasure of finding this room, I had not considered that. It is a worthy question. It might explain a certain sense of . . . what . . . something unique about Old Robin?"

Ambrose turned away from the books and faced Kiki. "So, back to me. You found them . . . my definitions . . . entertaining?"

"Yeah, 'entertaining' is probably a better word to use than the word 'funny'. I actually found some of them more sad. Like the one about love being a case of temporary insanity that can only be cured by marriage. I got to the age of twenty-three and never really had that kind of crazy love for anyone. Oh, I dated and had boyfriends, and some of my friends just lost their minds falling in love, but I never really fell head-over-heels in love with anyone or had anyone that crazy for me. And now it will never happen. I can still feel sad for that."

Kiki thought she saw concern in Ambrose's face. His silence seemed to be permission for her to continue.

She continued after a short pause. "We keep getting away from you, so here's some more I learned about you. I was in the library last night and looked up that short piece you wrote about what you saw at the Battle of Shiloh. It was so awful but it was beautiful too. It's weird. I guess what I'm trying to say is that I've never read anything with such beautiful words about such a horrible event. And you lived that?"

"I did live that. But you found my writing commendable?" Ambrose lifted one eyebrow.

"The part I can't stop thinking about was that part about all the leaves and branches of the trees being shot off and lying on the ground and then catching fire and burning up the wounded soldiers. I knew a boy in high school who died in Iraq but I never heard the story of how he really died. At the funeral they made his death seem like a glorious thing but nobody said anything about how he died. What you wrote made me wonder if maybe he died in some awful, horrible way and that nobody wanted to think about it. They wanted to think about . . . I don't know . . . make something wonderful out of him dying. There was nothing wonderful about dying in what you wrote."

Ambrose turned his attention away from Kiki to examine the books on the shelves. "I'm pleased that you admire my writing and now I will finally tell you something that I believe I know about this world. In fact, I am still here because of my writing. I stay because people still read my work. Such is the nature of my personal motivation. It gives me pleasure to remain here and know that some still read my writings. But more to your question, how any person actually stays here, I surmise, unfolds within two circumstances: The first is that you must want to stay here and not cross over. Since I find it rewarding to be here, I will stay as long as people print my books and as long as college students study me. If that sounds a bit arrogant, then let the accusation be recorded as a conviction. The final determination is that, under such circumstances, I am pleased to stay here."

Kiki persisted with her questions, following him around the room. "So, are you saying that if you cross over you won't be able to see people still reading your books?"

"The answer to your question is one that I do not know with any certainty, but I fear it, and thus comes the other thing about which I have some limited confidence in the knowing. At the point in time that no one finds me to be of sufficient interest to remember me and my work, I would have no option of staying. One stays here only as long as there is someone in the world of the living who holds you in their thoughts. Otherwise, one would . . . umm . . . and I struggle for just the right words here, but you simply fade . . . or . . . float away to the other side when there is no one left in the mortal world who takes the time to consider you a person worthy of remembrance. In the absence of attention by the living, the spirit is compelled to leave this place and move on to whatever and wherever it is that is the next destination." Ambrose ended his explanation with a dramatic wave of his extended arm, a kind of farewell gesture.

Kiki's face betrayed both sadness and puzzlement. "So, that's why it's not very crowded here. It seems that not many people get remembered for very long. Anyway, my parents are pretty young, not even sixty yet, so I guess I'll have the option of being here for a few years. After then . . . I'm an only child, so I'll . . . what did you call it . . . float or fade . . . after they are gone? It could be that *Mothers Against Drunk Drivers* will have my name in a book somewhere, but that's not a lot to hang around for."

Ambrose lifted his hand. "Here is another point, something I'm learning more about—and I stand convinced of it—no one is required to stay. All have the power to leave, to cross over to that final place, if it is indeed the final place. It is a decision one may make."

"But that all just seems so mysterious," Kiki blurted out impatiently. "If you decide to leave, how do you go? How do you make it happen?"

Ambrose replied with a detached air. "Indeed, I am still working on understanding that. I have no conclusions, only a few observations. Would you care to hear them?"

Kiki pled fitfully for him to continue.

Ambrose paused before he answered, his attention still split between Kiki and the books in the room. "First, you will find no children here. I sometimes see a few youngsters, ten or eleven, but no one younger. I observe that children, who

I have seen only briefly, always pass through quickly. Their faces are marked with a longing, perhaps searching for their parents. That is one possibility I offer. They clearly seem drawn to something other than what they have here, and then . . . they are gone, and again, rather quickly I should say. The similarity in the experience of the young might argue for some force, some power that guides them and pulls them along."

Ambrose could see that Kiki was hungry for more. He professed his hesitancy to speculate further because very little of what he believed rose to the level of certainty. He warned her that he could be wrong about some of this.

Clearly pleased with what she had learned about the spirit world from Ambrose, Kiki returned to the more personal line of inquiry. "So, you're saying that for you it's about staying around to see what people think of your writing. There's got to be more to it than that. Do you have other people you spend time with here? Do you have friends?"

Ambrose paused to consider the question before giving reply. "The concept of 'friends' is not exactly the same as that of the prior world, but I do have other spirits that I know about and spend time with. And I welcome their company, so I will forgo my reluctance and call them friends. All are like me. They lived long lives, if measured in mortal years, and they have been here far longer than the time they spent with a beating heart."

Kiki clapped her hands, showing excitement, although no sound came from hands absent mortal flesh and bone. "Can I meet some of them?"

"Actually, there is this old Buddhist man that you might like to know. Would meeting someone like that be pleasing to you?"

"Wow, a Buddhist? I can't say I've ever met a real Buddhist. That's so interesting. Such a mix of religions. How do you know which one is the right one? Is that something you have learned anything about here? Is that something that you would talk to me about?"

Ambrose puckered his lips and squinted. "I must encourage you to give that little worry. But since you are a business woman, I will give you a metaphor that perhaps will make sense. All the religions you know are the retail version, each with its own unique packaging and branding. Perhaps while you are here, you will get to see something of the wholesale version. But don't look to me as any kind of expert on the matter. It is probably accurate to say that I have taken my own advice in the matter and have given that very little of my attention."

"Okay . . . I think I get that," Kiki answered.

"So, we will begin with my Buddhist man?"

"I'll put it on my calendar." Kiki chuckled at herself for using words so often said in her last world, realizing that she carried no instrument or device one might call a calendar.

"One more thing," Ambrose asked before letting her leave. "Can you say some more about what was so good about my writing?"

"Well, when you ended the piece about Shiloh, I thought the last part of it was such beautiful words, and when you think about the part about Christians killing Christians . . . well, it was just such a contrast, I mean, that awful situation told in such beautiful words. That's about the best I can do. I wasn't an English major, so I don't express myself too well sometimes. Does that make sense?"

"I'm very pleased with the way you have read and understood what I was trying to communicate. Now let's go meet my Buddhist friend. We may just entice him to visit this house. It would be interesting to see what he thinks of all of our mysteries here."

CHAPTER 4

KIKI AND THE BUDDHIST

To visit the man who Ambrose named as friend required a short trip to an Episcopal church. Before entering, Kiki asked a question obvious to her, being a haunting agent: "Why would an Episcopal church be an appropriate haunt for a Buddhist?"

Ambrose gave an answer that Kiki thought could have come from his famous dictionary. "Episcopalians will accept anybody and anything, even ghosts, as long as they act like Episcopalians."

Before she could ask for clarity about the behavior of Episcopalians, an elderly looking man-spirit, dressed in a very long but simple tan robe, appeared in front of them. His smile lit his entire face and his eyes beamed a warm welcome.

"Hello, hello, hello. I sensed that someone was coming. My happiness is multiplied by finding one old friend and someone new." He placed his palms together in front of him, in prayer position, and bowed low. He lifted his head and tilted it to one side, maintaining his constant smile, and waited for the guests to speak.

Ambrose took charge of the introductions. "Hello, Sid. I did bring someone new to meet you. I thought it would be okay. I think you will find her interesting . . . and comfortable. Sid, this is Kiki."

"Your name is Sid?" Kiki asked, then added, "I wouldn't have expected a name like that. Maybe something foreign, or just different."

Sid glanced at Ambrose, then turned back to Kiki. "It is a name that your culture calls a 'nickname,' a short name for something longer." His eyes seemed to twinkle along with his smile. Ambrose coughed, clearly to stifle a chuckle (since spirits need neither to cough nor to clear their throats). Kiki noticed the gesture and accepted the fact that she might have been on the outside of some information and did not pursue the matter.

Kiki was energized and curious about the man before her. "Are you the only spirit here in this church?" she asked.

Sid replied, "I am one of the few who has remained, but I am not alone here. Often you may catch a quick view of a young man dressed in his best priest clothes. He is indeed a priest who died young. His name is Father Robert. He appears to be settling in for a long stay. He studies the church building itself as if it were a scripture. I would be surprised if he allowed you to engage him, as he may be struggling with his place here. He does not confide in me. He acknowledges me reluctantly." Sid's smile softened briefly and then again lit the room.

Kiki further lit the room with her enthusiasm. "This just gets more and more interesting. You'd think a priest would be eager to go to the other side. What's he waiting for? Can I just try to talk to him, too?"

Sid held up his hands but also bowed his head to show respect. "Slow down, my young friend. You just asked me several questions and we do not want to get too far ahead of ourselves. I see that our mutual friend, Ambrose, has been telling you about life in our world. Certainly, there will be a time to try again to approach Father Robert. However, as I said, our young priest seldom acknowledges the presence of others and rarely allows social engagement. But for now, what about you, young lady?"

Ambrose picked up the conversation, addressing Sid.

"Indeed, let us not miss my purpose for bringing you my new friend. You and I have marked on more than one occasion that we do not have the opportunity to enjoy the company of many young people for conversation. I wager that we both might find her company rewarding."

"Yes, yes . . ." Sid nodded enthusiastically, bowing several more times with hands folded, and giving the appearance of moving his weight from one foot to the other, despite not having weight in the usual sense of the word. He gestured with an open hand toward the pulpit in the front of the church, then waved his other palm along a path to indicate row upon row of polished wooden pews behind which the day's light streamed through stained-glass windows. "What is your interest, young lady? Do you want to see my little church here?"

Kiki had never seen anyone before who smiled so constantly and seemed so delightfully happy. "Well, not really. I've seen and been in lots of churches like this. I'm more interested in what you can tell me about being here as a spirit. I don't know if Ambrose has told you that I am pretty new here. How long have you been in this . . . uh . . . spirit world?"

"How long by what measure? By mortal clocks?" Sid replied.

Kiki was genuinely perplexed by the question. Ambrose pulled her aside and briefly explained that Sid had been in this world for far longer than Ambrose himself had been, if placed along the measure of mortal time. He droned on until Sid once again captured her attention.

"Ambrose loves to talk about time. I love to talk about time. I once caught time in a teacup—"

Ambrose jumped in again, addressing Kiki. "I hope you are ready for a lesson about Buddhism. Do you know anything about Buddhism?"

Kiki's eyes widened and she answered enthusiastically.

"I once worked in a T-shirt store and we had all these Buddhist quotes on the shirts. They were some of our best sellers. I can't remember many of them, but my favorite was about whatever your mind chooses is what you will become, or something like that. Our boss gave everyone a shirt with that saying on it. He said it made you a better salesman if you lived by it and you would sell more shirts."

For the briefest of moments, Sid lost the smile, then quickly recaptured it and spoke softly, chiefly to himself. "Generations of priceless wisdom printed on the front of a simple one-layered garment." He exploded into a laugh of pure joy and beamed at Kiki. "I like you! Welcome to our world. I hope you will stay for a long time."

"I just want to know why you have stayed so long," Kiki said in a serious tone.

Sid stopped laughing but kept smiling. "Okay. Here we go. Mr. Ambrose is right. I must give you the Buddhist lesson. Was there anything on those T-shirts about finding happiness through lessened desire?"

"I think I remember something about that, but not really. Yes, something about four . . . uh . . . lessons or something, the path to happiness . . . I can't really remember all of it."

Sid's beaming smile became wistful, almost gone. "I lived for many, many years in the world of rampant desire and ambition. I learned from wise, wise men that the path to peace is to give up the pursuit of possessions, of pleasure, of achievement, of earthly acclaim, and through that, all pain vanishes and one can live in this harmonious acceptance of life. It was so hard to do. I wanted so much. I hungered for fame. I particularly loved gold and silver. I ached with physical passion. I even tried to starve myself, just to flee from hunger."

"Wow," said Kiki, unable to disguise her enthusiasm. "I

really didn't get that from the T-shirts. I thought it was about setting goals and reaching for the stars. What you're saying actually sounds . . . what . . . actually a little lazy? I mean, if everyone just gave up their desires and dreams, who would accomplish anything? What if nobody ever wanted to be a doctor anymore? Who would take care of sick people? Would people still build houses?"

Ambrose moved to bring clarity to the discussion. "Kiki, I'm not sure you're quite hearing his—"

"Oh yes she is, my friend." Sid regained the floor. "She has it exactly right. Many, many things that mortals hold dear, those elements of the trophied life, would no longer exist. But that is my point. One must have faith that when all that ambition is set aside you are changed, but the key is that when all of that struggle is given up, then something better takes its place. As the Christians would say, you must have faith." Having lost Kiki's attention, Ambrose moved away to closely examine a stained-glass window.

Kiki became aware that these were conversations quite new and puzzling to her. "I just can't see it."

"I know. It has taken me a long time to see it. But let me ask you a question. When is the last time you wanted something good to eat or drink?"

"Not since I've been here," Kiki answered after a brief pause.

"Do you miss it?"

"Not really," Kiki answered cautiously, as if reconsidering her reply.

Sid continued, "Think about this. Since we no longer have bodies, we no longer need food, water, sex, shelter, money. We are in that state of peace and freedom from want."

"But we're dead!" Kiki gave her reply with more emotion than she had felt or showed since her death.

Sid moved directly in front of Kiki's residual form, wearing a smile that threatened to break into open laughter. "Are we? 'Dead' is such a problematic word. It is a concept only for a certain realm. Are we dead? I am here talking with you. I have spent more than a usual human lifetime here with my friend Mr. Bierce, who incidentally is no longer tortured by the need to produce written words on a page for the consumption of others resulting in monetary payment in order to sustain his wicked desires."

A smile now crept over Ambrose's face. "Are you sure I no longer have wicked desires? You might be surprised."

"Let me get this straight," resumed Kiki. "All your life you struggled to get to where you needed nothing. Without a lot of success. But now in the spirit world, you're there. Okay, I get it. I actually feel a little bit of that. But it still seems a little sad to me. Then again it sounds like you had a long, rich life. I didn't live long enough to have much or do much. So, anyway, you are now happy to stay here and to not want anything to own anything or look for anything to happen. Is that your story?"

"Happily! Happily!" Sid moved about the sanctuary with a quick dance-like motion, despite the absence of solid feet to mark the steps.

"Okay, then let me ask you this: What do you think is on the other side that so many people are in such a hurry to get to?"

"Not even I, the, uh . . . not even I know for sure what is on the other side." Sid looked down, an expression on his face indicating something akin to disappointment, or at least resignation.

Having remained mostly silent during the last of Sid's polemic, Ambrose impatiently chimed in. "Sid, you know a lot more than you are willing to reveal to our new friend. You are not showing her respect. Tell her what you think. Pray do not leave out the part about how most Buddhists believe in reincarnation."

Sid looked away, gave up most of the smile, and reluctantly began. "When I walked the earth in physical form, I doubted there was anything beyond the grave. I don't really know, but for many measures of human time I have had the growing feeling that there is something substantial on the other side. It is not emptiness and it is not merely another version of freedom from want and desire. On the other hand, I doubt it is a version of the Christian heaven, where one is reunited and restored and fulfilled in ways we might never have achieved when we walked on rocks and soil. But count my belief as also my fear that the other side may be simply the dock for the boat that takes you back for another birth, struggle, and death just like before."

Despite there being no need for earthly air for his spirit form, Sid ended his speech sounding breathless.

"And count me terrified of that as well," said Ambrose softly. "To return to war? Or worse? I could handle almost anything, even oblivion, but to be reloaded like a musket and shot back into the world? The way it now presents? With its 'modern' offerings? No thank you."

Sid also reflected. "Yes, the world is so different now from the many centuries ago when I moved within it . . . I, too, think it would be much more painful, so much harder than before. Men would crucify me or cut off my head!"

"You've been here for centuries?" Kiki asked.

"Twenty-five or so, by the turning of the earthly calendar, give or take a decade or two."

Kiki looked first at Ambrose and then at Sid. "Wow, this is a lot to take in. I thought I was coming here with a few pretty simple questions."

All three became silent, having for the moment exhausted the issue. Sid led the conversation back to more recent experiences. The conversation eventually turned to a review of the death of the man in the house Ambrose wished to haunt. Sid inquired about the current state of the dead man's spirit.

"That is a bit of a puzzle," said Kiki. "No one has actually seen Dave in the spirit world." She stopped to consider. "Wow! That's really stupid of me. I never thought to ask where his spirit is now."

Sid's face showed alarm. "Oh, this is very bad! His mortal body has been dead for more than a year and no one has seen or heard from his spirit. Very bad! Very bad!"

Kiki and Ambrose urged Sid to explain his concern.

"How death occurs can be important. Some spirits who die suddenly or in a tragic and senseless way have difficulty connecting to others in the spirit world. It may be a way of avoiding the truth. Tell me, what kind of ceremony was conducted and what was the nature of the goodbyes to the living construction of the man?"

"Well, that is the other thing," Kiki explained, speaking slowly. "Since he just disappeared, and no one found the body, and no one really knows what happened, there hasn't been any kind of a formal funeral service."

Sid looked shocked and continued. "Bad! Very bad! We know he is dead, but no one who is living and cares for him knows he is truly dead? No wonder he is lost. He is surely feeling abandoned. He's out there now, wandering in the air, trying to understand what has happened to him."

Kiki jumped in, "But I know where he . . . his body is. Do you think we should go there? Do you think we could figure out how to tell people where he is?"

Ambrose cautioned, "That would certainly be the right

thing to do, but we have no way of communicating to the living realm that kind of specific information. At least, I do not know how and I have yet to witness such a communication."

"Very difficult. Very difficult, but maybe not hopeless," added Sid as he turned to Kiki. "You seem to say you know where his remains now rest. Take us there. Without delay!"

CHAPTER 5

FINDING DAVE

T he three sprits traveled toward the place in the woods where Dave's body lay. As they moved, Kiki took the opportunity to find out more about her new world. She stretched out her arms and looked down at her form. "I'm still trying to understand about our bodies, or whatever you call this. I mean, we pretty much look the way we did the day we died, but there's no solid stuff. We can't touch things or move them around, but we look like we could."

Ambrose shook his head slowly. "There is so much about this I still don't understand. The common experience appears to be that spirits who remain here for any measure of time simply stop wondering about it."

"And what about the way we move? Our feet don't actually touch the ground, but we get from place to place, and sometimes we are high in the air, looking down at the tops of trees. I wouldn't call it flying. Floating, I guess."

Without looking at Kiki, Ambrose mumbled a reply. "The present arrangement seems sufficient for managing one's affairs, such as they are in this world."

Kiki turned away, not satisfied with Ambrose's answers, but aware they had arrived at their destination, an open meadow surrounded by tall pines and the occasional hardwood. Wild grasses had regrown on the spot of Dave's burial, and a few scattered leaves lay about, but if the area were examined closely, the observant person could discern an area approximately six feet long and three feet wide that stood out as lacking the mature growth of the grasses in the surrounding area.

Sid came out of deep thought. "So sorry. My concern for Dave grows, but what were you talking about?"

"Don't worry about it, Sid," said Ambrose. "Just some conversation Kiki and I were having. I await your revelation of the tool you are going to use to let the living know about Dave's resting place."

Kiki made a mental note of the skeptical and dismissive quality to Ambrose's words, but did not feel she had permission to speak of it.

Sid continued with no acknowledgement of Ambrose's tone of voice. He spoke in a peaceful, pleasant, somewhat detached manner. "First of all, Dave's not resting. Until someone knows that he is dead and where his remains lie, not much good can happen. I sense that he is not far from here, but he's too fragmented to make himself known. None of what we might say would make sense to him. But I do have an idea. Listen carefully. What do you hear?"

Kiki and Ambrose grew silent and listened carefully for several mortal minutes. "I hear nothing," Ambrose said, irritation clear in his reply. "There is nothing there."

"Shush, just allow a few more moments. You need not be so impatient. I trust there is no more important task you feel an urgency to attend." Sid's reply carried just the hint of rebuke to Ambrose, who turned away but kept silent.

After a few more seconds, Kiki spoke. "A dog. I hear a dog barking far from here."

"Yes!" Sid spoke in an excited whisper, and his smile exploded again. "I will call to it." He floated high above his two ground-level companions, arms open wide and head uplifted. A few minutes more and all three spirits could hear the barking of several dogs, running hastily toward their location. Human voices called from behind them, bidding them return, but the dogs ignored their masters' entreaties until they came to the place where Dave's remains lay quiet below the soil. Four hunting dogs milled around the spot, whimpering and growling softly, occasionally looking up into the air above them to where Sid hovered. None of the dogs barked at the hovering spirit man, nor did they clearly acknowledge the definitive presence of Sid, but at the same time there was, without doubt, something of interest in the sky above them.

Minutes later, the first of the men bearing rifles caught up with the dogs. He and the second to arrive looked puzzled and somewhat angry that their dogs had left the pursuit of traditional game. At no time did the animals point toward an expected quarry. But when the third man arrived, a more experienced hunter, he noticed what the canines had found, that distinct character of part of the ground that indicated something notable. Brushing away the leaves to show the clear delineation of the rectangular space, he said loudly, "Hell's bells. Bet you my best dog against a beer there's a body buried here. You got your cell phone, Jake? We got coverage out here? Call 911 and see if we can get somebody out here."

Kiki, Sid, and Ambrose remained to bear witness to the several days of the forensic process of recovering the body and a meticulous search for anything in the surrounding acres that would tell a story. Sid expressed his conviction that Dave's spirit would manifest at some point, now that his earthly vessel had been reclaimed.

The unfolding of this process was new learning for both Ambrose and Kiki, but Sid had seen it before. As they left the area, Sid told his companions that he sensed a presence, incomplete, still unwilling to engage. He expressed the belief that Dave's spirit was taking shape.

On the way back to the church, Sid assumed the role of teacher for his two companions. With one question following another, they speculated about the future of newspaper and television stories about the discovery and about how it might unfold over a longer period of time. Ambrose's mood now changed from reluctant and moody to eager partner, asking questions worthy of the journalist who once walked his human path. They agreed that, all things considered, this could be good for Suzanne Hurd. Now it seemed she could move on to the rest of her mortal days, and whatever else might follow.

"But we are forgetting one little detail," Sid added.

His two companions looked puzzled until Kiki broke the silence, "Oh my God! The two killers! Are they going to hear about this? What are they going to do? Do you think they will try to come back and get the money now? That can't be good news for Suzanne, can it?"

"Perhaps we should pay them a visit," replied Sid.

CHAPTER 6

TWO OF THE NICEST GUYS YOU COULD EVER MEET

Sid, Kiki, and Ambrose arrived at the home of the two men just in time to listen to them argue about retrieving the money hidden in Suzanne's house. Kiki gazed about the place, perplexed. "Uh, how exactly did we know how to find them, and is there a way to call the dogs in on them?"

Ambrose answered. "I think we had that conversation. It is indeed a mystery about how some things are known, and by whom. I told you my best guess, that some information just comes through the air, but it is a questionable supposition."

"Ambrose's guess is some approximation of the truth," said Sid with more conviction. "I have had the experience of simply wanting to know and waiting patiently for it to manifest. Let us collectively open our minds to the winds of memory and learn what we can about how they came here and what is on their minds. Some iteration of calling in the dogs may be a little more difficult to accomplish. Finding a body is a simple thing. Connecting it to other actors in this drama is far more complicated. We are at the mercy of future developments. But we can hope."

Barely an hour's drive in an earthly motorcar north of the excavated grave, two men sat in their rented house and saw the television reports about finding Dave's body. The older by ten years, a man called Grove, punched the air with his finger. "Tom, you saw that damn report on TV. They found our boy and dug up his grave. That grave is all over the damn Internet! And police ain't stupid. Bet you dollars to doughnuts that they snoop all over that house and find the money, now that they know there's foul play. You hear me? Police ain't stupid. That money will be gone and we're stupid for lettin' it happen." Grove moved closer to Tom, puffing out his chest to intimidate him as he always did when they argued.

Tom answered meekly, "There's no reason to believe anyone would connect finding his body to something hidden in his attic. We cleaned up good. No trace of us in that house." Tom spoke softly to not provoke the older man. He looked down at his feet and softly made his case. "Nobody's lookin' for us and nobody will connect his death to us. Money's safe where it is."

Grove paced and swore. Tom continued speaking in a soft and gently pleading tone. "Grove, now is the worst possible time to go messin' with that house. We got to wait at least until the story ain't in the paper no more. The TV and newspapers gonna be all over that house for months."

Grove seethed with anger but grew silent, his characteristic response when he acknowledged that Tom was right.

Grove and Tom had set up house in a small crossroads community quite by accident. After stashing the drug money and dispensing with Dave's body, they stopped to fill up their car at a one-of-a-kind convenience store on a rural southern Virginia secondary road. On each of three corners of the four-way stop stood large old farmhouses, all in various states of disrepair. In the front yard of one of the houses a handmade sign advertised rooms for rent.

As Grove finished filling up the gas tank, he looked wistfully at the scenery beyond. He turned to Tom. "I grew up in a place that looks a whole lot like this. Crummy run-down gas stations, rotten old stores and houses that ain't seen a paintbrush in years. You know, I think we should check out that For Rent sign. I could teach you how to fit in here if you don't try to show off how damn smart you think you are and start talkin' about things most people don't care nothin' about."

For once, Tom agreed completely with Grove. It looked to him like a place where no one would come looking for them.

They knocked on the door of the house that displayed the rent sign in the front yard. Lettie Hester welcomed the two men into her home and accepted their story that they were brothers from northern Florida who had just buried their father. Grove had his story fully formed by the time Lettie sat down with them around her kitchen table to talk about what she had available to rent.

With a mournful and humble look on his face and tone in his voice, Grove described their situation. "The tax man took what was left of Daddy's house and farm. I couldn't believe it how much debt he and our mom had run up. No way we could pay it, so now that land is gonna be some rich people's fix-it-up house. So, we're on the road, no choice but to try to build a new life somewheres else. But we ain't afraid of work. That's all we ever did. We just need a place to stay until we figure out what to do next. Most likely look for farm or construction work now."

Lettie led the two men upstairs. She laboriously took one step at a time up to where two small rooms stood open. "I hear you 'bout that tax thing. Iffin' you want to hear it I can tell you how the govament's got my neighbor's check all messed up. Her son's check too. It's a fine kettle they dealin' with."

A brief conversation between the three about the price of the rooms and the house rules led to a handshake contract. Lettie added, "And don't worry about references. I put more stock on what I can tell about people face-to-face than what others say about them. B'sides, you probably ain't gonna give me no names of anybody who would tell me not to rent to you anyhow, now would you?"

Grove and Tom smiled silently and followed Lettie back down the stairs.

"You know, ma'am," said Tom as they descended, "I do possess some decent carpentry skills. Know anybody who's hiring somebody who knows how to drive a nail? Or paint a house?"

Lettie shook her head. "Not right here, but they's a couple a little town mostly north and west of here where houses are bein' built. You might pick up a little job there. But iffin' you won't take no offense, I'd suggest you get a haircut and shave them beards. People 'round here still a little funny about how you look. And I'd say too, it'd keep people from talkin' about me and the people I rent to. Don't mean I won't rent to you, but like I say, people talk."

The suggestion that Grove and Tom change their appearance fit well with their own plan. As the parties were finishing the exchange of money and information concluding the agreement to rent, Lettie happened to mention that she used to cut her son's hair. Thirty minutes later she swept up from her kitchen floor the clippings from Grove's shoulder-length brown hair and Tom's even longer blond locks. She also, without actually asking permission, took a pair of clippers and a large straight edge razor to their beards. When Tom saw the size of the razor

and felt it gliding easily over his face and neck, he felt naus-
eated and his face flushed red. Lettie laughed at him. "Yeah,
my son and husband always used to look a little spooked when
I put this blade to their necks, but I never cut them . . . 'cause
they never gave me reason to." She chuckled as she pocketed
twenty dollars for her work.

Sporting look-a-like buzz haircuts a quarter inch in length,
the two "brothers" thanked Lettie and returned to their car
to unload what modest possessions they had packed. After
another trip back to the convenience store for shaving and other
supplies, Grove and Tom looked in the mirror to witness the
result of their transformation. They looked each other over and
agreed they had never seen the person they were now looking
at.

"I see why you had a beard," said Grove, "you got no chin."

"Kiss my ass. Your neck looks like a plucked chicken."

In the short term, the killers were not in need of money.
They had kept several thousand from their stash and used it to
pay the rent and buy new clothes. Then as the weeks passed,
they began the process of inserting themselves into the lives of
Lettie Hester and her neighbors.

Around the breakfast table and during early evenings sitting
on the back porch, they heard the story of each of the properties
associated with the three farmhouses clustered together within
a stone's throw of the others. Each had once spread out in
its own separate direction—north, east, and west—reigning
over successful dairy and grain operations. Competition from
large-scale agriculture and the fading interest of subsequent
generations spelled the end of all three farms. Most of the land
went fallow and wooded and was eventually sold to people
building houses. Lettie and her neighbors represented the last

of the original families who now lived in the big rambling farmhouses, getting by for now on money from the sale of land, and government help.

Grove and Tom were in time welcomed by each of the neighbors, one household made up of an elderly couple who needed yard help and had modest dollars to pay. Grove successfully reclaimed his southern accent, tempered but not entirely erased by urban life. A seeming fondness grew between the two men and their landlord and neighbors. Grove cut their grass, trimmed their hedges, and shored up a small barn that would have eventually fallen in if left unattended. Reluctantly, with a skillful show of modesty and gratitude, he accepted the occasional ten or twenty dollars in return for his work.

Tom took the car and drove away most mornings, saying he found small jobs in nearby towns. In reality, he mostly drove to a nearby rural state park and walked the trails alone.

In the third farmhouse lived a widow and her fifty-year-old son Albert, disabled from an illness the nature of which was not obvious, but manifest through his life of long, silent days spent alone on the front porch. Tom took an interest in Albert and sat with him, in conversation or in silence, many hours, rewarded with the occasional discussion about things read, places visited, and people Albert had known.

Within days of their arrival, Grove and Tom noticed a smaller abandoned one-story house at the back of Lettie's property. She explained it was a home built for her son who had promised to live there and eventually take over the farm. Her son's interest waned and he moved away to the West Coast.

Lettie and her renters agreed to a new arrangement for the men to move to the small house in return for their work to fix it up. Barely a thousand square feet, but with two bedrooms, this dwelling pleased the two, and had the other advantage of a small carport where their vehicle was more easily concealed from anyone who might come looking for it.

The elderly couple, the Franklins, had two children who lived a continent away but always came back for birthdays and such. One Sunday afternoon, Grove and Tom found themselves invited to the Franklins' fiftieth wedding anniversary. They attended without incident or apparent discomfort on anyone's part. They did leave early and someone asked Albert what he thought of Grove and Tom.

Albert said with a rare smile, "Two of the nicest guys you'd ever meet."

With the information of Tom and Grove's deceptive journey, Kiki spoke to her companions in a manner that invited discussion. "They've been there for a whole year and nothing awful has happened? Wow, I would have expected . . . but, I mean, I can't believe this is going to end well."

"Would you care to repeat your opinion that they are not intelligent people?" asked Ambrose.

"Well, I guess they're smart in some ways. The drug dealers haven't caught up with them and they haven't done anything totally stupid yet."

Ambrose persisted in his challenge to Kiki. "Perhaps it is in their incomplete command of the rules of grammar that led you to think them unwashed, metaphorically speaking. Grammar, as I see it, is *a system of pitfalls thoughtfully prepared for the feet for the self-made man.*"[1]

Kiki took the criticism from Ambrose as he intended it. Had she liquid blood flowing through an intact circulatory

---

1 The definition of "grammar" from *The Devil's Dictionary.*

system she would have flushed red with embarrassment. After considering how to respond to this hurt, then finding no adequate reply, and feeling puzzled why Ambrose would direct his ire at her in this way, she turned away and grew silent.

Sid broke in. "Okay, I think we can let this rest for a time. It is best we leave this place now. Our time here seems to be sewing some friction among us. Perhaps, my learned friend, you were looking for some acknowledgement of your cleverness." He beamed a full smile at Ambrose, as if to lighten and brighten him by the force of pleasantness.

Kiki reacted with surprise to the suggestion that they leave. "What do you mean? We can't leave this. So much is getting ready to happen, with those men going back to the house. I mean, how long will they really wait?"

"Agreed," said Sid. "Oh yes. Oh yes. But with twenty-five centuries of experience, I have found that it is not good to become . . . what is the proper English word for it? *Obsessed* with any one thing all the time." He turned to Ambrose. "I understand you have a new house in which to reside. Can we go there? Will you give me a little tour?"

"Indeed. That would be my pleasure. I know you have inhabited a great many more structures than I have, but this particular residence has some features that may interest you."

Kiki was not convinced. "We can see the house anytime we want to. Don't you see that Suzanne is in great danger? Can you, can we, at least keep an eye . . . or an ear—or whatever you use to know things—so we can at least know when things start to happen?

Ambrose replied with an authoritative voice. "Rest assured that I and my friend, Sid, will know when they are ready to enact their evil plan."

CHAPTER 7
RETURN TO THE HOUSE

As the three companions left on their journey back to Ambrose's new haunt, Kiki continued her questions about conditions in the spirit world. "I still don't understand all this about getting from one place to the other, and it just seems that we can go wherever and even whenever we want. Is that right so far?"

Ambrose shook his head. "Correct, my friend, but it is even more complicated. Travel by spirits from one place to another is essentially a function of thought and desire. It is also independent of mortal time. You must give up your assumptions that guided your coming and going in the world of the living."

When Kiki looked puzzled, Sid jumped in. "To be honest, this thing about time is one of those things none of us fully understands. We can't actually travel through time, or at least I haven't been able to figure that out, but if you are careful you can move within it and immediately be somewhere in the near future that you want to be. Perhaps skipping time is one way to say it, or more accurately, like speeding up time. But one must be careful. I once rose up high above this globe of rocks and sand, sea and storm, just to admire the grand scope of it and I lost the whole third century. Missed a lot of interesting Roman life, what you would call history."

At length the trio arrived at the house and found Suzanne and Carson in the library. They stood back to observe, despite knowing they would be unseen wherever they moved within the room.

Carson motioned with a broad sweep of his arm toward the wall of bookshelves packed with hundreds of books and a few decorative items. "Let's leave all the books here for now. Proposed buyers find filled shelves more attractive than empty ones. As for the furniture, you can remove most of it. Maybe leave a few chairs and side tables for sitting areas for a hint about how a new owner could see a room or two."

"And the piano?" Suzanne asked.

"Your call. It's a nice accent to a pretty large front hall. Are you going to keep it or sell it?

Suzanne spoke through tears. "Dave was the musician. But it's hard to think about letting it go. Would a buyer of the house ever consider keeping it? I think I like the idea of the piano staying here." The living pair walked out of the library, leaving Ambrose, Kiki and Sid to themselves.

Kiki turned to face both of her companions, a look of alarm on her face. "Is no one but me upset about what we are seeing here? We've got Dave, his spirit, lost out there in the woods, or fields, or whatever you call that. And here's Suzanne, who just seems to be moving along and has no idea what danger she could be in. What if those men come back and she's here? Are they going to kill her too? Are we that helpless?"

Ambrose and Sid looked down. They gave her no answer.

Kiki exploded. "Well then. Maybe I'll just get the hell out of here! You, Mr. Bierce, told me that we're in some kind of waiting period before we move on. What exactly is this place we're supposed to—what—cross over to?"

Ambrose looked across the room to Sid to see if he wanted to reply. Sid gave none. "I have no information to share. No one returns here from that crossing. I surmise it is the final destination. Allow me to add I have no courage of conviction about that. Thoughtful other spirits with whom I have discussed the matter declare it to be a universal truth, yet no one claims a definitive knowing."

Kiki continued, "So, how do you actually get there? How do you cross over?"

"I am still trying to understand this, and lacking any interest in making that journey, I am hesitant to explore the phenomenon. I fear I might get too close to some edge and fall over, metaphorically speaking." Ambrose chuckled.

Kiki was not amused. "But you must have observed—something?"

"What I have seen is simply a withdrawing into oneself, a kind of aimless moving around, speaking nonsensically at times, then fade, or float, and they are gone. I have no access to their thoughts. Only a few exceptions: I have seen some leave in groups of two, three or more, sometimes several members of one family. In that situation there is often a sense of joy or excitement. Sometimes they sing or pray."

Sid moved from his place on the other side of the library and came close to Kiki, palms together and head bowed. "Please. If I may. I think I can help here." Sid's expression asked permission. Kiki nodded.

"Mr. Bierce is giving you the best information we have. But I think he is missing the point. He is not addressing your real concerns. I doubt he has ever met someone like you. I have seen few of your ilk in all my centuries. I have met precious few who have maintained your level of concern for either the living or for distressed spirits. But let's go a little deeper here, my young friend. Have you ever heard that bit of poetic doggerel that goes something like, 'the world is unfolding as it should'?"

"I did," Kiki replied with enthusiasm. "It was one of our best-selling T-shirts." She saw Sid's smile vanish. "What? Did I say something wrong?"

"If I must accept the T-shirt as a vehicle for the expression of universal wisdom, then so be it. But it is odd." Recovering his focus, he continued, "Yes, in that form the saying is a somewhat recent approximation of an ancient truth, but we must change it fundamentally. The world is not unfolding as it *should*, but as it *must*. The world, the lives of humans, can be no other way. It is the nature of things. I embrace anything that points out the essential truths—the musts—of humanity. And by accepting these truths, one finds a sort of peace."

Sid paused. Kiki nodded. Sid returned her nod and continued. "It's like in baseball when something untoward happens and you just shrug and say, 'That's baseball'."

"Baseball!" exclaimed Kiki. "You like baseball?"

"Sid likes baseball, boxing, bullfighting, and all those manly sports," Ambrose said.

"Yes. I like all those things, but particularly baseball for the things they can teach."

Ambrose deadpanned, "Here it comes. The baseball, Buddhism, and time lesson."

Kiki took note of the sarcasm in Ambrose's statement but said nothing.

"Yes, oh yes, oh yes. Time in the world of Buddhism and the world of baseball share a great deal. But I will spare you the long version of Buddhist thinking about time. I will spare you the tortuous descriptions of Buddhism's consistency with the laws of the physical universe."

"And thank God for that," interjected Ambrose, sarcasm undisguised.

Sid acknowledged his quip with a slight nod of his head and a frown. "Mr. Bierce and I have had endless conversations about the relatedness of Buddhism to the science of his day, and of later days, to the extent we understand it. Those conversations are routinely rewarding to me, but I think not so much to him. I will give you the short form and you tell me what else you wish to hear."

Ambrose kept silent and made a circular motion with one hand.

"Okay, so I teach best with a story or an example. Consider a baseball game. Within it we have a story unfolding before us. To most, time moves in one direction. The game begins and moves to its ultimate end with a winner and a loser. But the unfolding of the game of baseball is not fixed to a mechanical timepiece. There is no moving hand of the clock. The game is not measured by time's passing. The end of the game is determined by the behavior and accomplishments of its participants."

"Right. I do understand all about that," Kiki jumped in, engaging with Sid's guidance. "The team that has more runs at the end of nine innings is the winner. Or extra innings if it takes more, but there is no time clock."

"Yes, oh yes, except that in theory, it is possible that neither team will move ahead, ever, and the game could go on forever. And in that case, all participants would remain forever in the present, the arrow of time holding still, moving neither forward nor backward. Imagine them fixed in eternal hopefulness, presented with repeated opportunities, avoiding the specter of loss and humiliation, spared the disappointments, or the joy, of a conclusive outcome."

"Here is where I grow frustrated with you, Sid," Ambrose put in. "I think you are quoting me and you never give me credit. Remember when I wrote that the present is *that part of eternity dividing the domain of disappointment from the realm of hope?*"[2]

---

2 The definition of "present" from *The Devil's Dictionary*

"I give you great credit, my friend, but the credit is for finding anew the words for an ancient truth, discovered many times by countless others. Like many truths, they are lost and forgotten only to be reclaimed. If it will gratify you, I place my hands in prayer pose and I bow to you for your rediscovery of this wisdom."

Ambrose rolled his eyes. "Very amusing, but we seem to have missed the point of you coming here, my friend. You were interested in this house, and did I tell you it has a name? It is named after Lincoln's horse, Old Robin."

"Oh my God!" Kiki exclaimed. "I totally forgot to tell you what I found out about the history of the house."

"Indeed. Another trip to the library?" asked Ambrose.

Kiki continued, "There was a book there about old houses in Southern Virginia. Old Robin had a couple of pictures and a little about its original owner. It was built close to two decades after the Civil War by a man named William Anderson Bibby." Ambrose lifted his eyebrows and gestured with open hands. "And who was Mr. Bibby? He must have had a connection to the president. Did he come into actual possession of Old Robin?"

"The book had some of that. He was the fifth son of a wealthy Maryland man who owned a big horse farm. It seems that the family legacy was for the oldest son to inherit everything and employ the younger ones, but Mr. Bibby was not interested in that life and was studying to be a lawyer when the war interrupted everything. Somewhere along the way, he joined Lincoln's staff as some sort of speech writer."

"It is entirely logical that a man who grew up with horses could be interested in Old Robin," Ambrose mused. "So, how did the fifth son get the money to build this?"

"That's the sad part of the story. Two of his brothers fought for the Union and died. Two others joined the Confederacy and only one came home, the fourth oldest. The father was apparently devastated and gave the inheritance to the two boys equally. Somehow our Mr. Bibby took his money, moved to Virginia, and built the house. It isn't clear that he actually ever owned the real Old Robin."

"Maybe just an homage to a president he worked for and admired," Ambrose reflected. "And a love for horses, I suppose. Is there more about Mr. Bibby?"

"He never married. No kids. The house has changed hands many times since his death in 1910." Kiki paused and looked around with a puzzled look on her face. "I just felt something strange. Did either of you feel that?"

"What did you feel?" asked Sid.

"Hard to put words to it," she replied. "I shouldn't be feeling anything. I'm dead. But I swear I felt a chill." She shrugged and shook her shoulders and took what would have been a deep breath, if earthly vapors still coursed through her spirit's residual form.

Ambrose cut in. "You know exactly what she is feeling, Sid. Your little plan to take us away just didn't work. I think you felt it, too. I felt that shiver that you so desperately try to avoid with your so-called enlightenment, but I think it's caught up to you now."

Sid looked away. "Bad, very bad. Now we're really in it and no one knows how this will work out." His voice trailed off, the last few words not heard clearly. Sid's smile was gone and he looked down, withdrawing from interaction with Ambrose and Kiki.

Kiki demanded, "Will you two please tell me what you are talking about? What is this 'shiver' or whatever so-called feeling you say we are caught up in?"

Sid regained his composure and his voice. "We have allowed ourselves to become too involved in the affairs of the living. We are not paying attention to the given order of our current world, to stay detached from the cares of the mortals. Our path should be to seek our own personal serenity, and in time move on. But now the pain of these living ones, their fates, apparently matter to us. I don't know exactly how we have fallen into this circumstance, but messages now arrive, we are being called, and we will not be free of them until these things are resolved."

"What things?" Kiki implored, showing even more emotion than she had felt since her arrival in the world of the spirits.

Sid stretched out his arms, palms uplifted, and with one hand motioned toward the door, clearly indicating it was time for the three of them to go. He spoke softly, his smile restrained. "It starts with Dave. His spirit is in trouble and he needs our help. We have been selected for some adventure, the nature of which is yet to be revealed."

CHAPTER 8

BRINGING DAVE HOME

T he rural and wooded part of southern Virginia where Dave had been killed and buried lay sparsely populated, but every mile or so stood an occupied home.

When Sid, Kiki, and Ambrose arrived at the location they saw a half dozen fire trucks from the local volunteer departments, an equal number of law enforcement vehicles, and a score of firemen, officers, and other onlookers both in and out of their cars all staring, transfixed, at the tops of a grouping of tall and mature pine trees. Some saw a fire. Some saw a bright, multicolored light flash off and on, and others saw a dark distortion of the tops of the trees, an area seemingly dead to light, like a vacant hole in the trees. Each visual phenomenon appeared intermittently, then vanished briefly, moving around high in the trees and accompanied by the howl and moan of a soul lost between dimensions.

"It is Dave. He is raging," Sid said matter-of-factly.

"He's what?" asked Kiki.

Sid continued his dispassionate explanation. "He is raging. Angry. Confused. He has some idea of what has happened to him but he is still fighting, still trying to make it be something different than it is. He is so angry he is what you would call 'delirious' in human terms. He is lashing out in every direction. His soul is on fire. Only when it is this bad can the living see and hear the struggle."

"What's going to happen?" said Kiki.

Sid reached out as if to put his hand on Kiki's formless

shoulder, then pulled it back as he spoke. "We have no way of knowing. But this is why interactions between those in the spirit world and the living are so problematic. It is a phenomenon that is unplanned, uncontrolled, and defies understanding."

Ambrose turned to address Sid directly. "So, are you going to do your little call-the-dogs kind of voodoo and bring him to his senses?"

Sid did not respond to Ambrose's manner, but stated simply, "This is far beyond a call to point of a simple but sensitive canine. I think it is time for you to use those skills you have been learning. This problem is beyond me. I am all about acceptance. You are the magic man, or seek to be."

"Could someone tell me what you two are talking about?" said Kiki. "What magic?"

Sid and Ambrose looked at one another, each wanting the other to explain, neither of the two spirits sure if they wanted to try to explain to her something that was complicated.

Finally, Sid spoke. "Ambrose told you he stays in this spirit world because he wants to feel adored for his creative works. That is only part of it. He remains forever the journalist and he is trying to investigate and understand some things. He has a curiosity that I do not share. He entertains the idea that we are not so helpless here. He thinks there must be a way to communicate with and even influence, if not control, the events of the mortal world."

"You mean like you did when you called the dogs to the grave?" Kiki asked.

"And that was a mistake. One of the few I've made here. But yes, he saw me do that kind of thing a time or two. But I disappointed him with the limits of my powers. He went looking for other spirits who know more, who can do more than I. He keeps telling me that he will tell me what and who he has encountered but somehow he can't get around to it."

Kiki turned to Ambrose. "So, did you find others who can do more?"

"It would take one of your short lifetimes for me to tell you all that I have seen," said Ambrose slowly with his gaze fixed and far away. "And since I do not really understand it, I will not attempt to explain it to others."

Kiki could not tell if he showed sadness and resignation or some kind of hope in the tone of his voice.

Sid broke the long silence. "So, we need to figure out if you have learned anything from your other mysterious teachers who can help this poor soul or if we should simply watch and let it run its course."

"What happens if nobody can do anything?" Kiki asked.

Sid spoke first. "These random, clumsy, and often desperate bursts of expression by a spirit can intrude into the lives of the living. Such occurrences are sometimes given wild and occasionally creative and fantastic interpretations by mortal observers."

Ambrose added. "He's saying that this is how a lot of 'ghost stories' come to be. This one will probably be close to the truth, since we have a killing and a grave story right here. I believe we are looking at the birth of a local legend, maybe a haunted forest."

Sid added, "Except that he won't stay here. If my friend here has no magic to fold him into the comforts of our present world, he will run from here, fly or float or drift to who knows where. At some other place he will be seen and interpreted as a UFO or mysterious mountain lights or a dysfunctional weather balloon. He may be trapped there, in a form soon unchangeable.

And eventually he will, most likely, cross to the other side, but it is not a comfortable transition."

"Will you try?" Kiki pleaded to Ambrose.

"I shall try. I will move in closer to see what is observable. I am unsure regarding any specific act on my part. Sadly, I seem to be ignoring the *imperative duty of forbearance.*"[3]

Kiki watched anxiously as Ambrose moved up and away from his two friends.

Within seconds, Ambrose moved above the trucks, cars, and people and approached the pine trees. He felt a sense of weariness and loneliness, colored by fear. He had felt this before, a century ago at a place called Shiloh, and another time at Kennesaw Mountain. He found himself directly in the path of the multicolored apparition.

Ambrose sensed terror, confusion, anger, the most dreadful sense of loss. Then silent weeping, a searing melancholy, then pain, desperation heaped upon hopelessness all flowed though him and around him. And then the growing shadow of another spirit nearby, and inexplicably, a sense of more than one other. Powerful others, watching. Terror magnified. The sense of a great wind. Falling. Spinning. A hand to hold. A hand holding his. Hands around his body. Many hands. His hands around another. Falling. Then quiet. Dark. Voices in the distance.

Someone in the crowd cried out, "Where did it go?" And another, "I don't see it anymore!"

---

3 The phrase "the imperative duty of forbearance" appeared in the short story "A Son of the Gods."

Sid, Kiki, and Ambrose floated with Dave above the crowd below them. Despite not knowing who now accompanied him, Dave slowly calmed his feelings of fear and confusion and did not struggle or try to flee. Kiki seemed to Dave more familiar and non-threatening than the other two. He looked directly into her face, searching for answers.

Kiki began cautiously and kept it simple but honest. "Dave, my name is Kiki. We are together here and we are safe. I know this is confusing, but we are in the afterlife. Do you understand?"

Dave's tortured expression made it clear that he did not understand. "Is this a dream?"

"No. I'm so sorry. But this is real. It's really happening. Can I ask you a question?"

After a short period of looking around to the side and behind him, Dave nodded. Kiki continued. "Do you remember two men coming to your house. Do you remember them hurting you?"

Dave's eyes grew wide and he lifted his hands to touch the sides of his head. "No. Yes. Yes, I do remember now. I remember that. I remember being in pain. I was terrified. Not now."

"That's all over now," said Kiki. "You are among friends now. What else can I tell you?"

"I want—what do I want? I don't know what I want." At length he sat still without further questions. He could not look away and focused his attention mostly on the spirit form who called herself Kiki, then finally at the residual image of light and shadow that was now his own.

Eventually, he spoke again. "I remember being up in the pine trees. I was hiding but I was also stuck there. I kept trying to call for help but no words came out. Then I wasn't alone and that was good. It felt like somebody was actually trying to do something for me. Somebody, more than one—grabbed me and held me. Who was that?"

Kiki spoke reassuringly. "Take your time. There's a lot to understand. This will take some time to understand what has happened and where you are."

"How long have I been . . . what . . . dead?"

"About a year."

"My wife! I have to get back to her! Can you take me there?"

In a soft voice, Kiki replied, "Your wife is fine. She doesn't need you to do anything. Actually, there is nothing you can do from this spirit world."

"There's nothing I can do? So, what am I supposed to do?"

"I think the best thing is for you and I to just spend some time together. I haven't been here in this world for very long, but I know some things. Let's tell each other more about ourselves. I'll answer your questions the best I can. I think that would be a good first step. That will help us decide what to do after that."

Fighting confusion, fear, and despair, Dave lowered his face to his hands and cried. Then startled that he experienced no actual touching of his face, absent solid flesh, or anything akin to watery tears, he looked back at Kiki and said softly, "Can you help me?"

"I know I can. I've been through this."

Sid and Ambrose stayed out of sight of Kiki and Dave, moving above and among the graves of the cemetery, reviewing what had just occurred. Sid asked, "What exactly did you just do there?"

Ambrose spoke slowly, haltingly. "I did nothing. I merely presented myself."

"There must be more to it than that," Sid said plaintively. "Tell me anything you can remember."

Ambrose appeared shaken and confused. He grew silent and waited. After a period of time less than the duration of the chiming of a clock announcing the midnight hour, he continued. "Sid, if I still held mortal form and carried concerns appropriate to that condition, I would not tell you what I am about to reveal, for you would mark me insane. But we will relegate such trivial worry to our former state of being. We are, after all, dead, are we not? A designation of insanity holds no curse here, I trust?"

Sid could barely contain his curiosity. He wanted to shake Ambrose and demand answers, but gave a patient reply. "If such a thing as 'insane' is what the mortals would call you, I venture you should have no fear, or shame, if that is what concerns you."

Ambrose turned to Sid, his words urgently pouring out. "It does not concern me. But I am perplexed. I have just now been confirmed of something that I believed, something I have been told and have seen in part, but that I struggled to fully accept and understand. Sid, we are not alone in this world, this realm."

"What do you mean we are not alone?"

"There are other spirits in this realm that I am quite sure never traveled in mortal human form. They are powerful and they are not like us."

Sid felt astonished, bewildered, even embarrassed that he had never considered such a thing. Ambrose had inhabited the spirit world for just more than the unit of time that the living would call a century. Sid had remained there for twenty-five of such measures. Sid marveled at this wholly new idea to consider. He begged for more information. "What is the nature of such . . . such . . . others who are not like us, who have not been mortal as we have been?"

"I only know that they are watching us. I have talked with other former human spirits who have sensed them and have been carried close to madness—and euphoria—by the experience. But I am convinced such spirits were there when I approached Dave. They caused whatever happened to happen. I took no action of my own accord. I take no credit for this eventuality."

Aware that he was feeling emotions unbecoming to an enlightened being, Sid could not believe that Ambrose could be attaining knowledge or experiencing something beyond what Sid himself had learned or lived, in this world or the previous one. Questions flowed from him in a pleading manner.

"So, does this have anything to do with the people you say you have been learning from?"

"In a sense, yes, but no. I see their limitations now. They were, in the main, a group of old Holy-Roller preachers who think they know how to control the world through prayer. They must have attained an awareness of the others on some level, but on balance they merely performed some carnival tricks for me. They are a sideshow to what I experienced today," Ambrose replied wistfully.

Sid's impatience grew. His entreaty bore a mark of doubt. "So . . . these 'watchers' as you call them, are they the kind of spirit like 'God sees the little sparrow fall' and 'Yes, Jesus loves me' or more like the watchers of the *Book of Enoch*?"

Ambrose read his friend's frustration and sarcasm and roared with laughter. "My God man, you are envious! Your humanity is showing! Where is your inner peace? Where's the smile?"

CHAPTER 9

GROVE WANTS HIS MONEY

Ten days after the discovery of Dave's body, measured by the turn of the human clock and calendar, Tom and Grove had made some progress toward a resolution of their argument about retrieving the money. Tom finally accepted Grove's opinion that they should do it as soon as possible, but he insisted they have a clear plan about when the time was right. Neither Grove nor Tom had paid regular attention to local television or newspapers, so they were unaware of the commotion attending Dave's rescue in the newly known haunted forest.

During the previous week they made multiple drives past the house and discovered that public curiosity about the house where the murder had taken place had clearly faded. Only the rare sightseer came around. No trucks from TV or radio stations sat in the driveway. There also seemed to be little interest by anyone in buying the house. No one went in or out and the information brochures in the small box at the end of the driveway stood untouched. One day Grove left Tom across the street from the house for six hours, hiding in a stand of bushes. He saw no one come to the door. The house seemed to be uninhabited. The two men reached the conclusion that it was time for them to rescue their money, and they set a date for their plan.

Grove woke on the designated morning and immediately felt

irritated that Tom had already dressed and left the house. He considered the possibility that Tom could betray him and retrieve the money by himself, but from the window he could see their car. Grove went into the kitchen and yelled out the back door but got no response. Overwhelmed by frustration, he reached into the back of the top cabinet shelf and pulled out a bottle of Jack Daniels, poured himself a warm half glass, and drank it down in three quick gulps. Within minutes, he felt a surge of confidence and energy that he lacked when sober. Serving himself another half glass, and then another, he left the house to look for Tom.

Grove walked to the side door of Lettie Hester's house and knocked briskly. Invited in, he found Tom in the kitchen sitting at the table with Albert, Albert's mother, and Lettie, all huddled around a computer laptop, with Tom speaking into a cell phone.

"Heyyy! What's going?" Grove joined the group with a cheerful greeting.

Tom gave Grove a frown and a shake of his head, but Grove didn't care that Tom knew he had been drinking. Grove's change of personality when drinking came quickly and unmistakably to those who knew him. Tom did not break his conversation on the phone or otherwise show an obvious reaction to Grove's state of mind. Albert rose to shake Grove's hand and offer him a seat at the table. He quickly explained that Tom had been helping him and his mother get some things straight with their Social Security accounts.

Albert stepped with Grove to the other side of the room, so as to not disturb Tom, and laid out the story. Tom had figured out that someone at Social Security had pressed the wrong key on a computer or put in the wrong code on Albert's information. The government records had Albert confused with his father. This changed the status of all three, including Albert's mother.

Official records had Albert dead, his father alive and 55 years old, and Albert's mother no longer eligible for her husband's benefits. Albert explained that Lettie's benefits needed some work too, and that he would work on that next.

Albert bragged to Grove. "Tom is a genius in talking to the government. He's so damn calm. I'd have cussed 'em out and thrown down the phone, but I think he's got it figured out and found out a way for fixin' it."

Grove hid his irritation that Tom was spending time on this problem. He smiled, proud that he could hide his intoxication. Filled with energy, cheerful, and with a heightened sense of importance, he kept quiet for a few moments, listening to Tom talk to the Social Security rep. Grove kept his thoughts to himself, including the usefulness of having the Social Security numbers of Albert and his parents. He easily managed some polite small talk with Albert and his mother.

Tom put his hand over the receiver and spoke to the others. "I'm on hold here, but I'm having a little trouble hearing with everybody talking. Grove, maybe you and Albert could talk on the porch? Please?"

Grove gave back a smile that lit up the room. "You got it, Tom. Come on, Albert. I'll tell you a story."

Lettie stood and opened the door for Albert and Grove. "Albert, why don't you take Grove over to your house. You and Tom sit on your porch all the time, but I never seen y'all including Grove. Make him your friend too. She watched out the window as the two men walked across the road to Albert's house, talking enthusiastically, interrupting each other in friendly conversation.

Albert welcomed Grove into his house, then to his room, and retrieved a key from behind a picture hanging on the wall. He carefully opened an eight-by-four-foot gun safe, the only piece of furniture against one wall. Grove looked at Albert's collection of antique firearms and gasped. His actual experience with guns came with modern firearms, but he knew most of what he was seeing. Several Revolutionary War-era muskets stood out, but almost as impressive were a World War II M-1 rifle, a Winchester repeating rifle from Indian wars in the American West, as well as several he did not recognize. Two drawers at the bottom of the case revealed a set of antique dueling pistols and other handguns with which he was generally familiar, but the name "Colt" did catch his eye.

"Wow, can I touch 'em?"

"Be my guest," Albert beamed.

Grove lifted up one of the muskets as gently and respectfully as if it were made of fragile glass. "How much is this collection worth?" Grove blurted out. Aware he might be asking something inappropriate, he added, "that's not a real question, I'm just impressed; I'm just sayin' you got a real treasure here."

"Well, really my father's treasure, but I guess it's mine now. I don't know anything about how much they're worth. All of these guns—'cept the Winchester and the Colt .45—have some kind of connection to the family. The muskets came down from a long time ago. The M-1 is just like the rifle my grandfather used in France and Germany. But I don't really know about the dueling pistols. I never knew my father had them until he died and I got to get into the safe."

Grove reached down into the drawer and picked up a large, markedly heavy pistol that displayed two barrels, one on top of the other. "Never seen anything like this. What is it?"

"Oh, that's a real rare gun. It's called a LeMat. That top barrel is for bullets and the bottom one shoots shotgun shells.

I think the story goes that this Frenchman made 'em for the Confederate soldiers, but not very many. If all the rebel soldiers had got ahold of one of these, the rebels would have won the war. At least that's what Daddy said."

Grove experienced a sense of desire, of coveting what he saw so strongly that he had to remind himself to breathe. Then he relaxed as he accepted that these guns would be his soon. For all practical purposes they already belonged to him. The details of how to make that work would not be that hard. He wondered if Albert had ammunition for the collection, but feared that asking directly might make Albert anxious or suspicious.

Grove asked in a casual, almost reflective way, "Humm, wonder how long it's been since any of these have been fired?"

Albert shook his head. "Well, I never shot any of them, and the only one I ever saw Daddy shoot was the Winchester. Not too long before he died there was this pack of wild Chow dogs that came around. He took care of them. I think it's the only gun he actually had bullets for. Got a small box left back in the drawer."

Grove also took note of a half dozen shotgun shells in the drawer where the LeMat was stored. *Breathe. Calm down. Don't get too excited. Don't give yourself away.* He forced himself to look away, to give the impression that he had looked at them enough and that this treasure trove of guns, both decorative and functional, was of limited interest to him.

"Thanks, Albert, that's a real treat to see these, but actually I just came up to find Tom. I need to go back in the kitchen and ask him something. I think we were gonna work on the car a little."

"Come back later and let me tell you a few stories about my

grandfather," Albert replied, his invitation to his new friend both genuine and eager.

"I will definitely be coming back here," Grove answered with equal enthusiasm.

Back in the kitchen, Grove found Tom had finished his telephone business with the Social Security rep. When Grove entered the room, Tom immediately got to his feet and moved toward the door. No one else in the room seemed to notice his discomfort as the two men said a quick goodbye to Lettie, Albert, and his mother, and walked back to their house. Tom walked ahead, not talking or looking at Grove.

Grove stayed only a step behind Tom, essentially entering the room at the same time. The whiskey bottle with significant residual still sat open on the table. Tom gestured with open palms to the liquor while shaking his head and spoke a single pleading word.

"Why?"

"Why not?" Grove said in a nonchalant manner.

Tom paused, took a deep breath, as if considering if he really wanted to have this conversation. "Grove, you know what happens when you get drunk. You get mean. Not loud. Not all stumblin' around, but you do hellish things to people when you're drunk." Tom talked in a quiet, calm manner. He added cautiously, "You know we can't go today. If you're drinking it just won't work. We'll go tomorrow. It's just as good tomorrow. Okay?"

Grove nodded as he eyed Tom across the table, an amused smile disguising his real thoughts about a plan to steal the guns. Then thinking about the fact that Tom was the only person he had ever allowed to challenge his drinking, he considered killing him then and there. Concluding that Tom was still useful, he reached out and replaced the lid on the bottle of liquor and returned it to the cabinet.

"Time to make some decisions, some *real* plans." He motioned for Tom to sit. Tom obeyed and Grove continued. "We got a lot of things fittin' together now. I saw what you were doin' up there. Any chance you got a copy of those Social Security numbers you were workin' with?"

"No. For what?"

Grove rolled his eyes. "Tom, you just ain't gonna make it as a criminal unless you let me teach you some things. You know that big, hairy dude in Durham? Guy with one eye that don't work? Guy like that can take those numbers and give us a whole new identity."

"I don't have them . . . the numbers."

"When can you get them?" Grove asked impatiently but did not wait for an answer. "Our boy Albert has a case full of guns that we can sell or make other good use of. You should see what he's got in there. A couple of damn muskets and—"

Tom's face showed astonishment. "Grove, what are you thinking? You're talking about leaving a trail behind us anybody could follow. Right now, nobody's looking for us. Nobody's got a clue that we are the people who killed that first guy and nobody knows about the money." He lowered his voice to a soft pleading. "If we start robbing and hurting people, they'll find us out."

Grove countered the argument. "But nobody's gonna connect the dots either. It'll be a totally unconnected, random crime. People will think it was an inside job, somebody in the family."

Tom spoke softly. "It will be an inside job. We're on the inside. How many people know we rent this house? And then if we're just gone, the police will have descriptions of us. From the old couple next door. Or the people at the party. At the store. We been in that store a hundred times. You can't kill 'em all, Grove. We can't take a chance that way!"

Grove became silent, unable to refute Tom's argument, then he spoke again, more to himself in a dreamy reverie. "But I want those guns. God, you should see them. You just never seen anything like them. They worth thousands of dollars. And we need a gun."

Tom gave a forced smile. "Grove, I need to ask you just one thing. Will you sleep on it? Will you trust me enough to just not drink any more today, get a good night's sleep, then tomorrow we go get the money and get the hell out of here? Will you do that, Grove?"

Grove couldn't really explain it to himself why he let Tom talk to him in this way. He thought about all the women and men he had beaten up when they didn't like his drinking. But in the end, he agreed. "Okay, Tom. That's fine. Let's just spend the rest of the day here gettin' ready to leave. We'll travel light. Couple of changes of clothes. Put ever'thing else in that dumpster behind the store. Leave early in the morning. I'll be outside on the porch thinkin' it through. No drinkin'. Promise. Okay?"

Grove stood up and walked out the back door to sit on the porch.

When night finally came, Grove slept a troubled sleep. A nightmare put him back in his childhood home. It began with real memories and grew to include present fears.

He was back in his father's house, a house that held a likeness to Lettie's home. Some features of Lettie Hester's house had been leading Grove back to those childhood memories from the day they arrived. It was the rain barrel and the cellar door.

At the corner of Lettie's house stood a rain barrel next to the door of a primitive dirt-floored cellar that once served to store canned food. Grove's home, when he was a child, had the same configuration of rain-barrel-next-to-cellar-door. Both became tools of discipline and punishment for young Grove. His father would save up a collection of Grove's misdeeds and wait until rain began to fall. Reciting Grove's sins, he would place the five-year-old Grove inside the rain barrel and scream at him, "It's up to God now! It's up to God whether you live or die! God washed the earth clear of sin once, and now he has the chance to do it again!"

Grove's father would pray and scream, cry and laugh, and then leave him there in the barrel with a final warning. "I done all I can. If God stops the rain before you die, then you have one more chance to stop being the sinful, evil, disobedient child you are. God have mercy on your soul!"

Most times the rain stopped soon enough; on too many occasions the rain continued for hours. The greater share of water from the roof of the house flowed directly into the barrel. Grove often spent eight to ten hours in the barrel alone, his hands just barely reaching the top of the barrel, holding on for his life, until his father would jerk him out and throw him into the dark cellar with a final warning. "So I guess God ain't gonna drown you. Now it's up to Him whether to send His serpent in down there waiting for you. I done prayed myself out for you and I'm done with your evil. It's aaalllll up to God now!"

As Grove became older and taller, the specter of death by drowning diminished, but he still spent time in the rain barrel and in the cellar. Each misstep of the child, from lost gloves to chores not completed, to sullen or fearful face in the presence of his father, was punished. His hatred for his father, and for God, grew stronger with each cloudy sky.

In his dream that night, Grove was back in the barrel, but this time it was Lettie's rain barrel. She appeared above him and for just a moment he thought she might be there to rescue him. Instead, she took up the cause of his father and screamed at him, accusing him of the most heinous crimes. In the space between sleep and wakefulness, as he fought through the night to fully exit the nightmare, Grove made a plan to kill her, to burn her house down on top of her and her son. It fit his plan for the guns. No one would think to count whether a gun or two were missing from a charred gun safe.

Tom slept little through the night. He watched through an open bedroom door as Grove struggled and tossed in his bed. He remembered the many nights and days he had stopped his father from beating his mother and his real brothers by simply staying calm and keeping his father talking and distracted. He called this his lion-tamer act. Today's show ended well enough. The lion had not pounced. Tom had survived up to now. The neighbors were safe, for now. It was going to be a long day tomorrow. He considered the consequences of doing something, or not doing something, with the bottle in the cabinet.

CHAPTER 10

TRYING TO PUT THE PUZZLE PIECES TOGETHER

For the next several days of mortal time—and who can say how long in the perceptions of Sid and Ambrose—the two spirit men talked, argued, occasionally taunted, and yelled at each other while trying to understand what Ambrose said he experienced when trying to help Dave.

"You know, you have an arrogant, cynical, have-to-be-right-all-the-time side of you," barked Sid.

"I will take that as your feeble attempt at flattery," Ambrose replied, "but I will say it is hardly a fitting statement from one of history's so-called most enlightened ones. Did they teach you that in Nirvana?"

"Nirvana is not a place. If it was, it is clear you'd have never set foot in it," Sid shot back sarcastically.

Ambrose was undeterred. "How is it you found such peace of mind and inner calm for all those years and now you appear to have lost it in full measure? Could it truly lie in the reality that I, a lowly commoner in your eyes, seem to have discovered something that you missed or ignored for twenty-five hundred years?"

"Something I missed or something you misinterpreted?" countered Sid.

The two men grew silent. Sid fought through emotions of anger and envy and quietly accepted that something remarkable happened in the encounter between Ambrose and the troubled spirit, beyond the capacity of either to understand it. Sid reflected on the fact that in the past when he had witnessed the raging of troubled and fragmented spirits he stayed apart and never knew how or if or when a positive resolution came about. It was not his concern. But now he could not turn away from the question. He silently chided himself for a lack of curiosity.

Ambrose drove the current argument on. "I'll finally say it. Are you aware that you have always treated me as—what—a child, an inferior mind? And are you aware that every time my writing is discussed you either ignore or actively dismiss it? And here we are at a time of what may be a remarkable discovery and you disrespect me with every word you say."

Sid puffed out his cheeks as if he were expressing real air through lips with skin and blood. He turned away and placed his hands on his hips.

"What about your so-called four noble truths?" said Ambrose. "I see nothing remarkable in them. Just an excuse to disengage with the world, and not in a unique way. The Benedictine monks figured out the same thing without your help, just called it the 'will' that needed to be tamed, what you called 'desire'."

"Not really," Sid replied with a dismissive tone. "The Benedictines were simply trying to hide from the world. Sure, every religion or sect or philosophy has heroes, but that group for the most part was simply looking for a free ride and somebody to take care of them."

"I must say you are remarkably comfortable showing disdain for the lives and thoughts of others. One might expect a modicum of respect for one of the world's great religious orders."

"At least I chose to suffer in my search for truth."

"Yes, 'chose' is indeed the key word," Ambrose spat. "You

had a choice, and in the end, you chose to stop suffering. You drank the nourishment offered when you chose to do so. What about all the people who had no choice? You were on a selfish journey of some kind of divine pity when you mortified the flesh, all because you were born with a silver spoon in your ass, if I may mangle a metaphor. This inner peace you found comes mostly from your desire to return to the loving and pampering arms of your mother when you were an overfed, overindulged, and . . . and—"

In that moment, Sid raised his hands, and with wide eyes, he said, "Look at us. We are indeed squabbling as children do."

Both men regarded each other, then burst out laughing in a sustained guffaw that, if they had been mortal, would have taken their breath. Had they corporeal shoulders and backs to hug and pound they would have embraced and fallen to the floor in happy, tearful mirth.

"You are indeed my friend," said Ambrose. "I once told someone that one does not have friends in this realm, but that is truly wrong, for I am yours and you are mine."

"Oh yes, oh yes, you are my friend and I am yours and I have an idea," spoke Sid. "We seem to have found ourselves in conflict about something having to do with the truth or the nature of human suffering. Let us go on a journey and talk about some things."

Ambrose and Sid moved and traveled within the medium that was the world of the spirits. They placed the entire world in their sights, and all events of human history. First, they took stock from high above the earth to see the blue and green orb in its entirety, then came closer to view the Asian steppe country where Sid first asked Ambrose if he knew of the history of Genghis Khan. Ambrose confessed only modest knowledge. Sid reviewed for him the story of the brutality, the cruelty, and the total humiliation and annihilation of enemies at the hands of the "Universal Ruler."

"So, what is it that is so illustrative about this time of history?" Ambrose asked.

"This time in the history of the world was not the first or even the last time cities were burned and common innocents killed, but it is a point in time that shows how utter the devastation of human life and human dignity can be. It is this capacity of the human condition, the fundamental human stain that still molds the actions of men now upon the earth, including our boys with the money in the attic."

From there they turned west, Sid invoking memory of the bubonic plague that claimed half the population of Europe, bringing civilization to a halt and a turn backwards followed by the slow grinding of an agrarian rebirth only to then suffer the waves of Viking invaders who took everything, killing everyone unable to flee quickly enough.

Ambrose listened but his demeanor clearly showed he was becoming impatient with Sid's polemic. "I grant that you have seen it all, watching it all for twenty-five centuries, in addition to your earthly spin. But I must respectfully ask: So what?"

Sid replied without hesitation. "I, for the first time, feel threatened and hopeful in equal measure, but this is not the outcome of my existence, it is not the destination for which I yearned. My hard-won sense of peace and tranquility that I cultivated through self-imposed denial and hardship, is nowhere to be found." Tears filled his eyes for the first time in many mortal measured centuries.

"But the horror you brought me here to see is not new."

"But don't you see? Until now I had an answer. I could be detached from want and still congratulate myself on my capacity for compassion. I had it figured out, until now."

"And by now, you mean the others, the beings I encountered," Ambrose replied.

Speaking with a voice that held both sadness and regret, Sid continued: "For some time now, I have experienced a sense of . . . of . . . something I cannot name. A feeling of incompleteness. All I have done, all I have learned, is not complete. And now you tell me of these others, these spirits you encountered, and I believe you met someone or something remarkable, perhaps something wonderful." He lowered his head, put his face in his hands for just a moment, then looked up and with no smile, indeed, with a pleading countenance. "And I crave the knowledge and the company of whatever and whoever you discovered. I covet it to the point that I feel I may burst."

Sid gathered himself and continued. "And I am now the supplicant to the man I have, as you say, disrespected. Let us now move on as equals."

Together they retraced every moment, every movement, leading up to the encounter in the haunted forest, during, and immediately after. They confessed to each other their fears, their hopes, and wildest speculations of who the others could be. Perhaps the others were "angels" in the tradition of the Christian God, or perhaps some entity encountered by humans in countless places on the planet and given interpretation and identity based on the culture of the observers. Perhaps the others were something new, something just now arrived from some other realm, involving itself or themselves in the affairs of humans and spirits.

Ambrose addressed Sid respectfully, "Okay, my friend, you took me on a journey, now it is my turn. What I am about to show you may or may not have something to do with what puzzles us, but I feel incomplete without my showing it to you." They again stood, or floated, or perched high above the great green and blue globe, surrounded in patches by the white vapors in the air, hurtling through space and time. They paused for a moment, or a century in their own mark of time, to consider the firmament. Moving back to near ground level, Ambrose steered them both to the mountains of North Carolina.

"Pray tell me what occurred on this path before us?" questioned Ambrose.

"Easy answer. It is the trail of tears, left by the expulsion of the American Indian Tribes from their homeland. Circa 1830s if I remember correctly," Sid replied.

"Andrew Jackson was not Genghis Khan, but which is the greater suffering? A quick decapitation or a march to oblivion?"

It was Sid's turn to be puzzled by the teacher. "I watched them both but I cannot choose. Is there a lesson here?"

Ambrose turned away and bid his friend follow. "No lesson, just a warm-up. Let's go a little farther south and a few decades forward in history." Ambrose led his friend to the side of another mountain. "Tell me what happened here."

"Now I am stumped. I can see some historical markers about an American Civil War battle. There is a large metal plaque supported by stone, and some cannon placed on mounds of dirt, but I fall short of omniscience. You tell me."

Ambrose told his story in dramatic fashion. "Had you stood upon the ground directly below us in late June of 1864, you could have seen the bullet strike my head and see my body fall and lie still upon the ground."

"Wait! You did not die here," Sid stated with certainty.

"Quite right, I did not die here, but I suffered. I *lived*. And that is the only modest point I wish to make. I *lived* this. With great respect for you, my only present true friend, you *watched* the uninvited suffering of humanity during life and for two and a half thousand years after death, but I *lived* this."

Sid regarded his friend, and despite the nature of the spirit realm where souls come to calm down before crossing over to what is next, and despite the natural process of diminishing human feelings, fears, longings, and desires that is a part of the spirit-world life, emotions flowed over him like the great earthly flood of antiquity. Sid felt sadness, compassion, and a longing to embrace and comfort his friend. He wondered about the others and what they might have to do with compassion. Was it compassion that drove Ambrose to engage Dave's fractured spirit in the haunted forest? And did such an act—by a man who previously appeared to lack compassion—bring the attention of other spirits?

Over the next few days—or was it years, measured by arbitrary mortal time?—two friends redoubled their efforts to understand this new information. They considered Sid's self-proclaimed insight about compassion made manifest, then rejected it as too simple or too obvious, then considered it again. They spoke rapidly, simultaneously, eagerly together for hours, or maybe for decades, if some physical tool had been keeping mark of the transitory motion of time. Soon after they had exhausted all possible new ideas and were beginning to repeat themselves again, Dave and Kiki reappeared in front of them.

"Whew! What a journey we've been on!" exclaimed Kiki.

"We just spent three weeks in Europe!" added Dave.

Sid and Ambrose withheld comment about the perceived length of time Kiki and Dave spent in travel. They saw immediately that Dave was no longer the frightened spirit at the time of his rescue.

"I'm interested in your trip to Europe," said Sid. "We were just there ourselves, momentarily."

Dave and Kiki looked at each other, each offering for the other to go first. She finally took the lead. "Well, it's like this. He asked me how he could ever repay me for the help I was giving him and so I just said for him to tell me about his life. One thing that came up was when he went to Italy and it got me real interested because, you see, I had never been there." Kiki's excitement and enthusiasm grew as she spoke. Dave regarded her with a smile.

Ambrose shot Sid a look. "I doubt she saw the same Europe we talked about when we were there."

Kiki continued, "So, we decided he would show me a place where he was once very happy, and that was Italy. And there was this one place that I just totally fell in love with. It's called Noli and it's not too far from Monte Carlo, you know, where all the money and gambling go on. God, you should have seen the limos at Monte Carlo, but anyway, that's not Noli." Kiki spoke with such passion and joy that had she been still burdened by human blood, skin, and bone she would have needed to at least slow down for a deep breath, if not sit.

Dave was smiling, almost laughing, at her. "Noli is a small fishing village that seems to be from another time. In the morning the fishing boats go out. In the evening the boats come back with their catch and the people of the village greet them at the shore. The fish are cleaned and then bought to take home, right there on the shore."

Kiki took back the floor. "And I swear to you, it's not a huge town but it has plenty of stores and places to eat, but I dare you to find one piece of clothes with a logo or brand name. No IZOD or Polo or Nike or any of that mainstream marketing stuff. It was all locally made and it was beautiful!"

"Tell them about the old church," said Dave. "The one that's a rug store."

Kiki raced forward with her account, "Oh my God. I don't really know why I loved it so much, but this one store that used to be a small church, a very old church, was no longer a church and it turned into a store for Persian rugs. I want to tell you I have never seen so many beautiful rugs in my life. And to me it just seemed perfect, an old church now having a collection of beautiful rugs that will just make your head spin."

"So," said Ambrose, "I take it you were not a world traveler when among the living?"

"A single girl, twenty-three years old from a poor family and no money of my own, I guess not." A frown then came over Kiki's face as she continued. "But you know, I'm not stupid and I like to go places and learn things. Back when I was alive, I always liked meeting new people. I still want to meet some more people here, people who have decided to stay, like you and Sid. I want to know their stories. It helps me think about what I'm doing here and understand all this."

Ambrose looked at Sid inquisitively. Sid looked back and, anticipating the thoughts of his friend, said. "There are other such spirits to meet. Some of them stay here, or perhaps I should say get stuck here, for reasons that are unfortunate. Shall we introduce her to Victoria?"

"Who is Victoria?" asked Kiki.

Ambrose placed his hands behind his back and lifted his head. "Let us make a small journey in order to watch some television with Victoria."

"Television?" said Kiki. "People watch television here? Didn't see that coming."

CHAPTER 11
QUEEN FOR A DAY

The party of four spirits returned to the Episcopal Church. On the way, Sid gave them a brief description of the woman who called herself Victoria Vandupont, her last name being one she chose for herself after entering her current world, but it was what she insisted everyone in the spirit world use to address her. The middle part of her mortal life had been spent with a wealthy husband, traveling the world in the company of captains of industry, politicians, and the occasional member of European royalty. Her husband died bankrupt and penniless, and she spent the last decade of her life reluctantly and bitterly accepting the hand of charity in a slow descent into social and personal isolation. Her own death in the land of the living passed with little attention from the larger world.

"Victoria is not a simple-minded woman," Sid explained. "She is quite intelligent and resourceful, but she is not very insightful about her own circumstance and way of being in our world. She had some bad luck. Day to day she gets by. Yet she is stuck in the spirit world doing the same thing over and over again, and as far as I can tell, she has no wish to cross over or to change anything about her life . . . Or rather, her current circumstance."

"What does she do?" Dave and Kiki asked simultaneously.

"We'll show you." They entered a small office room of the church, one with a sign on the door explaining the room was designed and maintained there for the use of the presiding bishop of the local diocese. Although small, the combination of office and living quarters held ornate furnishings including a rolltop desk and built-in bookshelves that overflowed with leather-bound works and stretched from floor to ceiling on two walls. A small single bed outfitted with simple, unadorned linens completed the furnishings.

In one corner of the room, in a large wing chair placed in front of a television, sat a woman spirit of mature but otherwise uncertain age. Her clothing clearly suggested wealth and modesty: long skirt and high collars. She faced away from her guests and did not acknowledge them until Ambrose addressed her.

"You are looking most lovely today, Victoria," Ambrose announced.

Victoria rose from her chair and turned slowly, neither startled nor in lesser measure surprised, and held out her hand, palm down, as if expecting one of the guests to at least take it if not accept the opportunity to grace her hand with a polite kiss. Ambrose and Sid bowed together in what proved to be for Victoria an acceptable greeting.

"Your timing is impeccable," Victoria continued. "You always said you would come here and watch one of my shows with me, and my favorite is just about to begin." She motioned to the television with one hand and with the other gestured for them to join her. She acknowledged the presence of the two newcomers to her home, then put her hand to her ear and leaned in to the television to call attention to an eager and dramatic voice coming over the air, announcing, "From the Earl Carroll Theater on Sunset Boulevard in Hollywood, this is *Queen for a Day!*"

Dave and Kiki exchanged quick glances, clearly not sure how to relate to the new spirit in the room nor to the fuzzy black-and-white offering on the television screen. Before they could comment or question, Sid and Ambrose took up positions on either side of Victoria's chair and motioned for Dave and Kiki to do the same. Ambrose defined the situation with a soft whisper to the two younger guests, "We should not interrupt Victoria at the beginning of this show. I will explain later."

Seeing puzzlement in the expressions of Dave and Kiki, Victoria took it upon herself to explain what they would be seeing by giving a timely set of brief commentaries as her beloved show unfolded on the screen. First, the voice of the host of the show, Jack Bailey, rang out enthusiastically, "Would *you* like to be queen for a day?" Victoria then explained in parsimonious phrases that there would be three female guest-contestants, all with tragic stories. Each in turn would be interviewed by Mr. Bailey.

Kiki, in an audible whisper asked, "Is this a real show? You're kidding me. Right?" Ambrose and Sid simultaneously put finger to lips and frowned Kiki into silence. Dave and Kiki shrugged with shoulders and eyes and settled in to watch the program. Ambrose wondered silently whether this was a mistake, getting this collection of people together.

Jack Bailey introduced the first contestant. "Our first guest vying for the crown and scepter is Ann from Portland, Oregon. Her sister was involved in a tragic automobile accident and is paralyzed from the waist down. She needs a great deal of individual care, most importantly a specialized bed to assist her caretakers with her daily routine. Ann has traveled here at her own expense, bringing her three children with her because her husband is disabled as well and there is no one left at home to care for the young ones."

The camera zoomed in to reveal a sad and tearful middle-aged woman, then panned to a boy and two girls, all younger than teenage, all looking around curiously, one pointing excitedly at their image on the in-room monitor. Jack Bailey continued, "But Ann is not asking for anything for herself. She says that she and the Lord are doing just fine taking care of her own family. All she wants is that bed for her sister."

Dramatic music punctuated the narrative and the audience erupted with applause. Victoria took advantage of the break in the action, as the station went to commercial break, to explain that after hearing all three stories, the audience would make it known through an applause meter who among the guests was most deserving of the title of "Queen for a Day."

As the program resumed and Mr. Bailey began the interview with contestant number two, Dave offered a quiet whisper to Kiki. "This is like a sick *Wizard of Oz*, if you ask me." Frowns from Sid and Ambrose redirected their attention to the show. Victoria did not hear Dave's comment, or she at least pretended to not hear. Dave quietly mouthed to Kiki, "This might be *the* original reality show."

Finally, it was time to have the audience vote with their voices and clapping hands. Victoria proved correct in her own choice and her prediction of who the audience would find most worthy. Jack Bailey's voice boomed from the television, "Number one, Ann from Portland, Oregon, you are our Queen for a Day!" The audience broke into applause even louder than the cheers that brought her the prize. Ambrose and Sid both smiled, bowed to Victoria, and made a dramatic clapping motion with their hands in acknowledgement of her choosing the winner.

Hands covering a face full of tears, Ann from Portland walked to center stage where two stylishly dressed attractive women draped the royal robe over her shoulders, gently fixed a crown upon her head and placed the scepter in her right hand. They led her up a short walk of stairs to the queen's throne and invited her to see what prizes she had won. The sound of "Pomp and Circumstance" rang out as she completed her ascension to the throne and many generous prizes, including the bed she asked for.

Kiki moved away from the others and out into the hallway. Sid followed her and spoke. "Victoria once had all of those luxury items and she lost them all. This is the way in which she is stuck. She is angry, disbelieving, and sick at heart that she was once a queen and then it all went away."

"There's got to be a way to help her get past this. It's just—"

Sid held up his hand, signaling Kiki to stop. He spoke with his face directly in front of hers, and in a manner that caught her attention. "I have to say, young lady, things have not been the same since you came here. I have borne witness to Victoria's way of life for decades now and have grown comfortable with it. I have accepted it. Yet you upset my comfortable resting place. Thus, I have a question. Do you wish to pursue this further?"

"What do you mean? Pursue what, exactly?"

Sid interrupted Kiki, impatience undisguised in his voice. "Young lady. Forget that show for a moment. I have been less than fully truthful with you about something important. There are reasons I stay here, in this middle world, reasons that I have not revealed, and there is one specific thing about Victoria that intrigues me. Are you game for thinking about this?"

"Try me," Kiki answered with a tone of voice that indicated irritation and fatigue.

"How do you think Victoria gets the television turned on? I think you have been aware that we spirits are not able to reach back into the mortal world to communicate with the living or manipulate objects, including things like the knob that turns the television channels."

Kiki frowned. "Except that time in the woods."

"You have no idea how much that event is the exception to the rule. Certainly, there have been unusual and remarkable occurrences, such as with Dave when I called the dogs to a fortunate discovery. Yet those are rare, risky, and might be best described as happy accidents. Centuries pass without such events."

"So, what is the thing with Victoria, and how does she turn on the television?" Kiki asked with a tone that should have been matched with an eye roll.

"She does not turn it on. The Bishop leaves it on for her."

"Huh? That would mean she, as a spirit, can some way communicate with the Bishop, a man who is alive?"

"Yes. Something like that. He knows she is there, living in the office set aside for him. I was here once to hear him giving very specific instructions to the custodians that 'for security purposes' the television should always be left on and turned to the channel that re-plays old, vintage TV shows."

"She told you this?"

"Not directly. A little of it from Victoria, but I learned about the instructions for the custodians from a happy accident of simply being there."

Kiki's frustration evolved to a visible pout. "Okay. I get it. But what is it you want from me? What do you want me to do?"

Sid resumed in a gentle and patient voice. "Victoria doesn't like me. Somehow, she lumps me into all the men who have ever mistreated her, disappointed her, and left her penniless. She has this funny gentleman-and-the-lady act she does with Ambrose, but I don't think she likes him so much either, so she never talks to either of us about important things. Maybe if you spend some time with her you could find out more about her ability to communicate with the Bishop?"

Before Sid could elaborate, Ambrose appeared in the hall

beside them. "I hesitate to be the one who interrupts your cheerful conversation, but I do need to tell everyone that there is information . . . in the wind."

"I have been feeling it too," added Sid. "Time to go."

"Felt what? Time to go where?" Kiki asked.

Ambrose answered, "Our boys are on the move. It appears they are on their way to reclaim their ill-gotten treasure."

All eyes then turned to Dave as he joined the others in the hallway. He knew nothing recent about Grove or Tom and their current activities or location. Ambrose read on their faces a collective concern that telling him might be delicate. An uncomfortable silence and uncertainty descended on the group.

Dave saw them looking at him. "What? Is something wrong?"

Kiki answered. "We have to go to your house. There is something there that needs attention."

"Well, if you must, but I can't think of anything that would make me want to go back there."

The other three were not surprised at Dave's comment. Kiki, and to a lesser extent the two men, had seen Dave's shock and grief after he was rescued, but a fading concern with the living seemed to be the usual process of adjusting to the spirit world. His reaction seemed appropriate.

Dave confirmed their expectation. "See, Kiki and I have talked about this endlessly. If I understand all this correctly, I have been dead for a little over a year. My wife is moving on with her life and I have no way of being a part of that life. I have no way of influencing that life. I will say that I loved her totally when I was living, but right now I don't really know what that feels like and . . . I hope this doesn't sound awful, but I don't really care about that life anymore."

Kiki turned to address Ambrose. "That's the feeling I was

telling you about not long ago. My parents are moving on with their life and that's great, but what does that life have to do with me? I can't talk with them, I can't help them, and they can't talk to me or do anything with me, so why even go there?"

With precious little additional discussion, Dave announced he would not go with Sid and Ambrose. Kiki made the decision to stay with Dave. Neither had ever been to Alaska, so after polite goodbyes and thanks, they floated away in a northern direction, according to the traditional and arbitrary markings of the great sphere of sand, sea, and rocks that humans called the Earth.

After Kiki and Dave's departure, the two remaining spirit friends looked at each other silently until Ambrose broke the silence. "I dare say we are caught in equal *share of our common weakness*, my friend. We seem compelled to go and watch this abomination play out."[4]

"And what exactly is this common weakness? Perhaps it is a separate fate we worship? I once would have understood your going to such a thing as simple and honest voyeurism, having little to gain than the knowledge of some human occurrence, but I think it's more complicated than that. Are you merely a journalist of the continuing affairs of men? Or are you again thinking of the 'others' you talk about?"

"I will confess my interest, but I will not allow you to define my motivation, old friend." Ambrose spoke with a half measure of the tension and struggle that colored their prior disagreements. He resolved to avoid their previous conflict. "But it is indeed the others that draw me there."

"And the same is true for me as well. You are right, it is a

---

4 The phrase "share of our common weakness" appeared in the short story "A Watcher by the Dead."

common quest, a weakness if you say it is, but I choose to call it something else."

"Define your true motivation, man!" Ambrose erupted with a full-throated challenge. "I wish only to know their nature. I fear you wish to join them as a god!"

"A god? How dare you!" Sid moved around Ambrose as if pacing. "I am not and never was and never will be a deity. I simply want to regain the peace I once had. The peace I had for two thousand years before you came along and brought . . . brought . . . what is it you have brought here?"

Ambrose realized he was dragging Sid back into an unrewarding and unneeded conflict and stopped himself. He held up his hands, palms toward his companion, and lowered his head. "I am sorry, my friend. I see no cause for conflict. Accept that I am simply flawed and imprudent. Shall we just go and find out what is going to occur at Dave's former home?" And with that, the fight was over. They traveled easily and promptly to Suzanne and Dave Hurd's house where they waited for the car carrying two living men to arrive.

CHAPTER 12

GROVE AT WAR

T he alarm clock finally ended a restless night for both men. Tom had kept watch over Grove to make sure he did not go to the kitchen cabinet for the remainder of the alcohol. When the alarm woke Grove at the appointed time, well before daybreak, Grove insisted that Tom take a bath, pointing out correctly that Tom looked dirty and smelled worse. Grove made a show of telling Tom that he was going outside to make sure the car was ready for the trip. Tom rushed to complete his bath and entered the kitchen before Grove returned. A quick check of the bottle in the cabinet found it undisturbed. He waited in the kitchen until Grove came back and did not leave the other man's company until they were packed and on their way.

In the brief time it took for Tom to bathe, with the outside world still cloaked in the darkness of night, Grove walked quickly to Albert's house and let himself in the unlocked kitchen door. With a small pen flashlight, he quietly but purposefully made his way through the house. He found Albert in his room, sleeping soundly, and stood over the sleeping man for several seconds, knife at the ready, making sure he was truly sleeping.

Grove removed the key to the safe from its hiding place, took his time to quietly open the doors, and then chose several of the weapons from the collection. He clenched his teeth and silently cursed. He wanted all of them but knew he could not comfortably carry more than the Winchester, the LeMat, and the M-1 away with him. He replaced the key and closed the safe, then moved carefully out of the room with the pistol tucked into his belt, a rifle in each hand, and the pen light held in his mouth to show his way out. He silently congratulated himself for his stealth and efficiency.

Stepping outside, he stood beside the rain barrel and cellar door, a half-moon overhead shining through a break in the leaves of the large oak trees, providing just enough light to illuminate his path. No lights were on in the house or in the two others that stood nearby. No one had been disturbed. He pronounced the lot of them stupid for not having a dog to at least bark at an intruder.

Grove leaned the long guns up against the cellar door, walked over to the barrel, and shook it gently. Water sloshed in the bottom. Memories from childhood and visions of the dream where Lettie stood over him raced through his mind. Brief nausea grew into anger. Anger turned to a gripping sadness. He closed his eyes tightly, shook his head, and breathed deeply.

From his back pocket Grove retrieved a wad of gasoline-soaked cloth he had tucked inside a sealed plastic bag. He opened the bag to smell the scent and feel the wetness of the liquid on his hands and looked around for the most strategic corner of the house where a fire might kindle and spread. Draping the cloth over a small stick, he lit the cloth and watched it burst into flame, flaring up more quickly and strongly than he expected. He watched the fire consume most of the cloth and walked back to the rain barrel, dropped the burning remains into the water, paused, and waited until the smoke cleared, the flame fully extinguished. Looking up at the moon, he sobbed softly for just a few seconds, composed himself, picked up his guns, and left.

Tom and Grove left their rental house at 6:00 a.m. and treated themselves to a Waffle House breakfast an hour later, not far from the house that held their money. Grove started to leave a $100 bill as a tip for a sad- and stressed-looking waitress, but then agreed with Tom they should avoid doing anything that called attention to themselves. They left a modestly generous but otherwise forgettable gratuity.

As they completed their drive back to retrieve the cash, both clean-shaven, dressed in trim knit shirts and khakis, Tom tried to reassure himself that Grove had not had more alcohol. But Grove's mood, his attitude, his continued bravado and grandiose statements about what he was going to do with his share of the money frightened Tom. His companion sounded like the intoxicated Grove. Tom's fears leapt when Grove reached under the seat and pulled out the LeMat pistol that had belonged to Albert.

"Got us a little insurance policy right here," he said as he raised the pistol just high enough for Tom to see it but not be seen from other cars. "Couldn't find any bullets for the top barrel, but it did have a few shotgun shells, so we are locked and loaded and ready to go."

Tom held his tongue on all the questions he had. *What had Grove done to Albert to get the gun? Where did he get the alcohol? Did he understand that if they hurt anyone else it could ruin everything?* He knew if he challenged Grove, no good would come of it.

"So, tell me how you want this to go down. I mean, I think we jus' want a clean and simple getaway, yes?"

"Yessiree, Bob! That is certainly what we want. When we get there, we'll walk up to the front door like we are house hunting, just to make sure the coast is clear. Look at one of them little brochures in the box for a minute. Then we'll drive down the street—there's a little side road we can park in—and walk back to the back door. We'll kick it in and even if an alarm goes off, I'll be up those stairs and back down in two shakes of a rat's ass and we're clear! I figure any police comin' to the alarm will be ten, fifteen minutes." Grove was talking loudly. "If we do have any trouble, I got my get-outta-jail ticket right here in my hand."

Tom's mind raced. He considered jumping from the car or waiting and then running away as soon as it stopped at their destination. But he knew Grove was capable of killing him if he ran. He was also aware that he had no place to run to. He had bought in all the way with Grove. He had no other options. In the end he would honor the sense of responsibility he had for Grove. Someone needed to be with him when he was drunk. Someone had to be there to try to tame the lion.

Approaching their destination just before 9:00 a.m. at Old Robin and its large lot, fifty yards or more from others on either side, they came up behind another car. It slowed, then signaled and turned into the driveway where they were going. Realizing their plan may be changing, Grove kept driving past the house. After rounding a corner out of sight of the house, he turned around quickly in hopes of getting back in time to see who was going into the door. As they slowly drove past, they caught a glimpse of Suzanne Hurd entering the front door, recent mail and the day's newspaper tucked under her arm, a large purse hanging over her shoulder.

Not even having driven fifty yards past the house, Grove executed a quick three-point turn and drove back, pulling the car into the driveway behind Suzanne's vehicle. "This is so perfect!" he said. "Give her two minutes and she'll have any alarm shut off. We'll knock on the door like we're wantin' to see the house. We'll be in home free!"

Tom pleaded, "What do you mean 'perfect'? This is crazy!

What do you think you're going to do with her? We'll come back later; she probably won't stay long!"

Grove ignored the questions. He got out of the car and reached into the back seat, retrieving a small roll of duct tape and stuffing it into his pocket. "A burglar's essential tool, one of them," he said as he smiled at Tom. He walked over to Tom's side, ordered him out, and told him to get two of the information sheets out of the box left by the real estate agency. Tom obeyed, telling himself that there was no way he could not stop this, but maybe he could influence Grove in some positive way. He reminded himself to stay calm. *Don't aggravate the situation. Don't inflame the beast. This could still work out okay.*

As soon as Suzanne opened the door, Grove pushed through and had his hand quickly over Suzanne's mouth, dragging her to the floor. Tom obeyed Grove's order to close the door and lock it. Tom watched in horror as he spoke to her. "Okaaaay, little lady, nobody's gonna get hurt here. Just stay calm and we'll be out of here 'fore you know it."

She stopped struggling sufficiently for Tom to follow Grove's instructions about how to bind her hands and feet with the duct tape. Tom saw the terror in her eyes, but she did not fight, did not cry out. As Grove put the duct tape over her mouth, Tom spoke to reassure her, making it clear she would be able to breathe, she would not die, and the best thing she could do was just wait and they would be gone in five minutes. He pulled her over to the piano and duct-taped her ankles to a piano leg.

Sid and Ambrose perched at the top of the stairs, in the same spot that he and Kiki had stood a few weeks before.

"Do you think he intends to kill her?" Sid asked.

"I cannot imagine an alternative," Ambrose answered, then posed a question. "Tell me, friend: do you feel compelled to stay and watch this? Indeed, do you in any way long to intervene?"

Sid answered patiently, "The urge to intervene is not something that compels me. I have watched far more gruesome things. What about you? Are you wishing to have some path to her rescue, in the way you came to the aid of Dave? Be careful what you wish for. That event occurred entirely in the spirit world, except for three sensitive canines. I've never seen a direct intervention of the sort you suggest from spirit to mortal realm. It would require actions for which we have no resources, no capability to actually reach back into the living world."

Ambrose searched his mind for a practical answer. He wished for a course of action but found none. "Even so, I confess that I do feel discomfort. Despite my acceptance that it is *a problem the solution of which would bring me greater satisfaction than advantage*, I wish for options. I know it cannot be as simple as when you called for the canine discovery of the grave. Nevertheless, let us follow upstairs and see if opportunity presents."[5]

Grove and Tom left Suzanne tightly bound and taped to the piano, and ascended the stairs to the second floor.

"Tell me what the hell we are going to do with that woman!" Tom whisper-shouted at Grove as he dutifully followed.

"Will you just shut the hell up? I think we'll just take her out to the woods and put her in the same damn hole we put her husband in. But we'll have ourselves a little more fun with her than we did with him, if you know what I mean, before we're

5 The phrase "problem in the solution of which there would be greater satisfaction than advantage" appeared in "The Secret of Macarger's Gulch."

finished with her." Grove laughed again, the kind of laugh that Tom knew was fueled by intoxication.

"We can't do that!" Tom pleaded as he moved a safe distance away from him. Grove reached up and pulled down the ceiling ladder that led to the attic, then turned to Tom with rage in his eyes. Grove grabbed Tom by the front of his shirt and pushed him against the wall. In one hand he held the same knife used to kill Dave Hurd. Grove sputtered out an angry stream of curses, telling Tom that he would kill him then and there except that leaving his body behind would make things complicated. He demanded that Tom shut his mouth and do exactly as he was told. Tom whimpered his assent.

Grove then pushed Tom to the ladder and pointed with the knife up into the attic. Tom reluctantly ascended the ladder and Grove followed. The attic space was large but of a simple rectangular arrangement with only one chimney close to where they hid the money. Grove gave Tom an unneeded push toward where both men remembered they put the money, behind a section of wallboard. Grove wedged his knife between the seams of two sections and pulled one off. The briefcase with the money lay propped and undisturbed against the inner wall. Grove looked at Tom and smiled. "It's finally ours. Now we can start to live. You know I'd never hurt you. Let's just take a quick look at it and be on our way."

Tom nodded cautiously. His mind raced, seeking a way to placate Grove and spare the life of the woman downstairs. He closed his eyes and leaned against the chimney.

As Grove lifted the top of the briefcase, he stopped with mouth wide open, eyes unbelieving. This was all wrong. He had expected dozens of neatly bound packs of United States

$100 bills. He saw $100 bills, but the words on them spelled out "Confederate States of America." The bills were crisp and new and tightly packaged, but these were not the bills that the two men had placed there. Grove frantically fumbled through all the packs of paper money. No United States of America currency, all Confederate money. All had the same designation and the printer's location of Richmond clearly inked on each bill in the briefcase.

Grove had no way to understand this. His only explanation was that Tom had betrayed him. He thought of Albert and all of his Civil War guns. Albert and Tom must have schemed to put this together. No wonder Albert slept so soundly while Grove opened the safe. They were not going to put this ruse over on him.

He screamed at Tom. "You son of a bitch! What kind of trick do you think you and that bastard Albert can pull on me?"

"What are you talking about? There's our money right there. Just like we left it."

Grove screamed at him and then lifted his knife above his head and drove it hard with one motion into the middle of Tom's chest. Blood gushed from the wound with every beat of Tom's heart and colored both of them red as they fell to their knees facing each other. He lost consciousness within seconds. Covered with Tom's blood and disgusted with the mess he had created, Grove pushed him away, leaving the knife protruding from Tom's chest.

For the first time inside the house, Grove felt panic, confusion, and loss of control. He jumped to his feet and scrambled across the attic room. He fell once, spreading Tom's blood across the floor. He stumbled, almost falling, back down the retractable stairs. On the upstairs balcony overlooking the area where he had left Suzanne Hurd, he staggered, then pulled himself up by the rail, his only thought to get to the car and leave. Steadying himself at the top of the stairs, he looked down and saw something bewilderingly different from what he expected. His terror magnified, he rubbed his eyes, trying to change what unfolded below him.

Grove saw before him an open field, open sky above him, and spreading out in all directions an encampment of soldiers that he recognized to be from the Civil War era. It seemed to be early morning, not yet fully light, and men were in the process of awakening, eating breakfast from large cooking pots hung from iron tripods, dressing themselves, and seeing to their weapons and ammunition. On a hill close by on his left stood a tent surrounded by the starred and striped flag that hung unmoving in the still air. Young men moved leisurely in and out of the tent; occasional bursts of conversation around dying campfires punctuated an otherwise quiet gathering.[6]

Suddenly the limp and lifeless flag seemed to lift itself into the air, accompanied by a dull and distant sound like the growl-bark of some great animal. The ground shook. All men stopped what they were doing for just a moment, then sprang to their feet. Soldiers dressed quickly; the messcooks lifted the hot camp kettles from the fire and stood by to dump them. The camp swarmed with combatants who moved to assemble as the officers rushed from their tents. A mounted soldier appeared from nowhere and sounded the sharp, clear notes of his bugle crying out with a command, a call to arms, that was picked up and repeated, passed on to and then by other bugles reaching

---

6 This paragraph represents an appropriated and paraphrased description of the battlefield of Shiloh, written by Bierce in "What I Saw of Shiloh." The reader should take note of the similarity in plot lines between the short story, "An Occurrence at Owl Creek Bridge," and the story presented in this book.

off into the distance, beyond a line of nearby woods to unseen valleys.[7]

Sid and Ambrose, positioned just behind him at the top of the stairs, watched the scene play out before them. Sid turned to Ambrose and asked, "Are you doing this? How . . . are you doing this?" Ambrose looked directly ahead and said nothing. He dispassionately watched a scene of bewildering familiarity, with no understanding of how it appeared before him. Sid turned his attention back to the scene unfolding before them.

To his right, Grove saw a swampy area, and just beyond, a river. While any observer, spirit or mortal, would have testified that Grove now stood transfixed and not moving at the top of the stairs, in Grove's mind he ran toward the river, away from the soldiers, away from the higher tree-covered land where he glimpsed lines of dark shadows moving like demons toward the assembling soldiers of the encampment. The air grew loud with thunder and the earth trembled and Grove fell. Steel blue smoke came wafting down the hill obscuring his view of the river. He stood, then fell again, then rose and half walked, half crawled in the direction that he hoped would take him from this terror.[8]

At the riverbank he could see two small steam-powered boats, one leaving and filled with retreating soldiers, another arriving empty to load desperate men, many fighting each

---

7 Ibid.
8 Ibid.

other, a few trying to keep order as others leapt into the water to claim a first seat aboard the vessel of their salvation. From the high ground *the battle burned brightly; a thousand lights kindled and expired in each second of time.* Brilliant explosions magnified the growing morning light, casting the limbs of trees in dark silhouette, and flames burst all around. Occasional voices of men rose in cheers announcing a momentary advantage or partial triumph.[9]

The smoke lifted enough for Grove to see beyond the two rescue boats where two Union gunboats laden with cannon joined the fray. Each retort shuddered the ships as if they might tip, but wood and iron remained steady and rained down hell upon the advancing enemy. The battle seemed to slow to a standstill and Grove huddled in the high grass of the marsh, listening all day to the sound of small skirmishes. Night brought an end to most action, but Grove found no rest. The gunboats fired occasional volleys all through the night as Grove sought a path to some place of greater safety.[10]

He moved randomly. Hidden in a hollow and behind clumps of bramble bushes, he came upon large tents dimly lit by candles. Two by two, men carried inside litters bearing the wounded, some emitting low moans, some who ceased to moan and were carried out the other end of the tent to join the dead. A steady stream of men was welcomed in; a steady stream of men were sent beyond. Elsewhere the night was black-dark and it began to rain. Still Grove moved and at one point fell in with a group of soldiers, none of whom paid him any attention despite his lack of the accoutrements of soldiering. This was a beaten regiment, clothes soaked, hair dank, faces white, crying

---

9 Ibid.
10 Ibid.

out from time to time for food or water, in an absurd plea. They found partial shelter in a great grove of trees decorated with Spanish moss. Lightning strikes lit the faces of the men and Grove found some feeling of company and comfort in their shared suffering, but had no words, no thoughts to explain where he was or what was happening.[11]

A morning bugle called the soldiers away. Grove let them leave and made his way back toward the river. The rain had stopped. He moved through a part of the forest where the slow, persistent, almost infinite blasts of cannon and rifle had shredded the trees. First the leaves, then small limbs, and later the larger branches had been mulched into a fine kindling that covered the forest floor. Previously fallen leaves caught fire first then cooked the new fuel to burning point, resulting in a hissing glow of fire, steam, and smoke. Grove stepped down into the ash left from this fire and sank halfway to his knees. His right foot struck and exposed a soldier who had been roasted in this hell. Grove could see this was not a man who had died quickly, the body was twisted in agony that told of the tormenting flame. As Grove sloshed through the ash now made mud by last night's deluge, he came upon body after body with clothing burned away along with hair and beard, revealing hands formed into claw formation and a hideous grin of death upon their faces.[12]

Frantic, running and falling and crawling, Grove finally made his way to a high point on the bank of the river, just downstream of the boats and the fighting. He made one last glance over his shoulder and could see the boats bringing fresh troops from the far side where yesterday the others had

---

11 Ibid.
12 Ibid.

fled. He looked up at the high tree-covered ground and saw the advancing ranks of the other side moving forward like an endless snake crawling from the forest. He looked down into the river and saw it as his only hope to escape. He would jump into the river and let the current take him past the fighting. There must have been others who have done this, he thought. He took a deep breath and launched himself into the moving water.[13]

From her place on the floor beside the piano, Suzanne had watched Grove come down the stairs from the attic and pause on the balcony above the great open room. In her own world of terror, she knew he was returning to kill her. Her frightened mind could make no sense of what happened next. After rising from where he stumbled at the top of the stairs, Grove looked down toward Suzanne, took a single deep breath, and leapt headfirst from the ten-foot-high balcony. His head struck the side of a heavy glass-covered end table, splitting open his head and dislocating a vertebra in his neck. He died instantly.

Five minutes passed with Suzanne lying on her side on the floor, frozen in her continued terror, looking directly at the man who had jumped from the balcony. A small flow of blood pooled on the floor and spread out in her direction. She allowed herself to hope, but she knew that two men had gone up and only one had come down. She listened, heard nothing, and tried to put her mind to how she would free herself. Eyes closed, a prayer on her lips, she struggled against her bonds. Ten minutes passed as she desperately pulled on the tape around her hands. She seemed to be stretching the tape and her left hand moved

13 Ibid.

ever so slightly, but her shoulder ached and she felt exhausted. Pausing to rest, she heard movement upstairs. She looked up and saw Tom standing on the balcony, drenched in blood, one hand covering his chest, and in the other, a knife. He began an awkward, slow descent down the stairs.

Suzanne closed her eyes, made a last prayer to her God, and waited as she heard Tom grunting and breathing heavily, scraping against and smearing blood on the wall as he continued down the stairs. Opening her eyes one more time, she saw him reach out toward her with his knife. She closed her eyes, waiting for death. She felt the knife cut through the tape on her hands, then through the bonds on her feet, and then he tumbled down and landed across her body. She shouldered him aside and finished the job of removing the tape and frantically rolled and crawled away from him, wiping his blood from her arms and clothes. She scrambled to her feet, running out into the yard. Seeing no one around, but seeing no one chasing her, she went back into the house and reassured herself that both men were dead. She calmed her desperate mind enough to make the necessary calls for help.

The two men-spirits had not moved from their viewing place through the entire sequence of events. Sid turned to Ambrose and spoke in a whisper, "You did that. I know you did. How did you do that? Tell me!"

"I did nothing. I simply allowed myself to be a part of *the pitiless perfection of the divine, eternal plan.*" Ambrose turned away and left the house, far from view of anything else that would transpire that day in that house, and he told Sid they would discuss this later after he had some time for reflection.[14]

---

14 The phrase "pitiless perfection of the divine, eternal plan" appeared in "A Son of the Gods."

CHAPTER 13

SEEKING ANSWERS

The following day, or some approximation of a turn of the sunlit spinning globe, Sid and Ambrose made their way back to the forest where Dave Hurd had been buried and from where his remains were reclaimed. Ambrose had said nothing about his experience, or as Sid would have it, his role, in the deaths of Grove and Tom. Sid kept steady companionship with his quiet and distant spirit friend and quickly moved through curiosity, to disappointment, and ultimately reached acceptance that Ambrose would speak of these things when he was ready.

It was Sid's idea to return to the place of Dave's killing, and at length Ambrose questioned him. "Why are we going back to the forest?"

"Because I do know a thing or two, and if I show you that I'm not useless and stupid maybe you will tell me what you know that I don't," Sid replied, an expectant if less-than-radiant smile on his face. Even within his acceptance of Ambrose's unwillingness to engage, Sid's soul still burned to understand what Ambrose had experienced.

Ambrose gave reply, speaking slowly, giving weight to his anticipation. "Yes, it is quite remarkable. I have no idea what you are going to show or tell me. This process of how or why things are known by some but not by others remains bewildering. I expect you will show me something about Kiki and Dave and then I will have no rest until you have drained me dry of all I have learned, or think I have learned."

"Partly right," Sid came back quickly, "except I know nothing of our two young friends. The last I heard from them they were off on another tour of some exotic part of the planet beyond the narrow confines we have chosen and found comfort within for ourselves."

Ambrose spoke with a calm monotone, not entirely consistent with the content of his reply. "I am surprised and a bit worried about them, especially Dave. Do you think he should know about what just happened to his wife?"

"I think he does not care," said Sid without hesitation. "Have you not learned or do you choose to not remember what happens to these young adults when they come here? They lose interest in the mortal world. I have long concluded that this is a key part of the process of moving to the great unknown. My friend, you and I have had numerous conversations about that before and you seem to keep forgetting. You've actually talked about it yourself. Do you remember?"

"Assuredly. You are a wise man. I learn and relearn from you. And I am a troubled man," Ambrose continued in his monotone, his dark and brooding mood almost palpable.

"Troubled? What in the air, my friend? How is it that you are troubled?"

"Ever since young Kiki came to our world, I have felt that rarified feeling of concern for the feelings and experiences of others. It is quite unsettling. Then when we were last in the house and watching that gruesome eventuality play out, I felt a distinct feeling of nausea. How is it that with no corporeal gut to expel nonexistent food that I can feel nausea? I am perplexed and vexed in equal measure."

"That is very strange, very strange, my friend. No answers. Only questions. But can you leave your preoccupations long enough for me to show you what I—"

Ambrose cut Sid's words short. "I am almost ready. First I must confess something else."

All remnants of the beaming, constant smile that Kiki had noted on the face of Sid left him entirely. He spoke with undisguised irritation. "Okay, my self-absorbed friend, keep going on your own internal, infernal, interminable, and self-serving rumination. What is it in your private world that is so much more important than a gift I am trying to present to you?"

Ambrose came back earnestly. "No. It's not that kind of thing. I just wanted you to know that for the first time since I have been here, for the first time in over a century, I have written something new."

"You have what?" Sid sputtered out his bewilderment. "You narcissistic fool! We have watched this horrific human drama play out and I am eager to show you something about it . . . and my heart and soul burns to learn what you did back there—what you did and how you did it—and you tell me you can write again? For God's sake, man, tell me what it is so we can move on."

"I have written what I will call a commentary." He burst open a smile that covered his entire face.

Sid exploded. "A commentary? What does that even mean? A commentary! You take this time to tell me you have written something? When I have just watched something, and you have just manifested something that I think has never happened in recorded or unrecorded time and I am burning to know what you know and . . . and . . . I have been here twenty-five centuries and have known others who stayed here centuries more before they moved beyond but never have I been more . . . more . . . I cannot even name it, what you are doing to me now! Tell me about your damned commentary!"

Ambrose looked at Sid with peaceful eyes, showing no

acknowledgement of Sid's distress, and said, "Not now. Later. It wouldn't be right. I'll tell you later. What were you wanting to show me?"

All measure of peace and tranquility of the soul attained by Sid during his twenty-five hundred years of striving for self-consciousness and enlightenment vanished with their interchange. Sid threw up his hands, let out an audible groan, then lowered and shook his head as if to shake something out of his brain. He appeared to take a deep breath, despite the fact that he no longer drew actual air in or out of physical lungs.

Ambrose persisted with his peaceful smile. "I'm ready now. To see what you have to show me."

Gathering his thoughts for the change in topic, feeling some relief of his frustration, Sid motioned for the two of them to continue into the forest and approach the general vicinity where Dave was killed. Silently the two spirits regarded the forest from the same vantage point as on their original trip there, when Dave lay beneath the soil.

"Do you hear that?" said Sid.

Ambrose paused, said no, and then said, "Wait. I think I do hear something. It's very soft. It's a low kind of cry or groan."

"Keep listening," Sid instructed. They held silent vigil for several earth-measured minutes.

Ambrose broke the silence. "If I were compelled to compare the sound to a human event, I would say it is a man trying to awaken from a troubling sleep, a nightmare of some kind."

"Now I will call you wise, as you have said I am." Sid paused. "For that is exactly what we are hearing, my friend, but not from a human—from a lost spirit."

"What spirit . . . I mean who? Is Dave back in the woods that we have called haunted?"

"Not Dave, my friend," spoke Sid. "It is the man who is called Grove."

Ambrose showed genuine interest. "Grove? How is it that Grove is here? I mean, why would he come here?"

Sid's smile was back. "Aha, my friend, now you are questioning me. You think I have something to offer you. You think I know something that you want to know. As I know that you know something for which my soul burns for you to reveal to me!"

"Yes, yes," said Ambrose impatiently. "I am curious. I have already called you wise. Please go on and tell me about Grove now."

Sid quickly picked up his narrative. "Grove has returned to the place he felt most powerful. His killing of Dave was, for him, a supreme act of control and dominance over another. It gave him a feeling he never experienced before in his sad life of pain and powerlessness. This place drew him back through a power I do not fully comprehend. His spirit returned here but now lies spread out and shattered throughout the land surrounding the grave."

Ambrose kept silent but his expression marked intense interest.

Sid continued, "Yet Grove does not understand any of this. He does not know how he has come to be here. He is incapable of the most rudimentary consideration of his situation. Even more salient, he has no insight into his very nature, so he will be here for a long time. He will growl and moan as the ghost of the haunted forest for a very, very long time. At present he does not even possess sufficient form to move from here to any other location. This I have seen before."

Ambrose considered for a moment. "And although I did

not plan or intend for this to happen, I fear that I have been the instrument of putting him here."

"That is what I want to know," said Sid. "What did you do! How did you do it! Tell me, man, I tremble with excitement about what you are about to tell me."

Ambrose came fully out of his disinterested musing. "I do not know what I did, or at least I do not know how I did it. Yes, all that you saw displayed below us when we stood upon the balcony in the house, all of it was my memory. It came from my experience, preserved in my writing, and Grove had the misfortune to relive it when he fell from the upper floor to his death. But this was not my idea to do that. It was not of my volition."

Sid could not stop himself from interrupting. "So . . . someone or something else used your thoughts, your experiences, and placed them in the other man's mind, and in ours for us to witness. For some purpose! For some purpose! That's the key here. There was a guiding hand at work here. For a purpose!"

The two friends paused just long enough to prepare a thought that came from each simultaneously. From Sid it came as a question; from Ambrose, a declaration. "There was someone else there!"

"You felt a presence of another there?" Sid asked. "Yes, you did, I know you did. I did not, but I know you felt it. Tell me, man. This is what I have stayed here for all this time, the measure of so many human lifetimes. I knew . . . I hoped . . . it would come to this. I suspected there was . . . what . . . a divine presence? Did you see anything? Did you hear any sound? Did you have a communion with the higher power, something that we might call holy? Speak!"

"The word 'divine' does not ring true, at least in the way that any of the religions have proposed it. I saw nothing.

I heard nothing. What I felt there was a powerful, but not a confident, being. It was definitely someone or something other than myself, but its nature was that of a pleading, not a leading. It seemed to be asking me for help, for guidance, and for my strength to use for its ends." Ambrose smiled at his friend. "If I still held human form and craved the feel of air within my breast, I would ask that we leave this place and breathe some fresh air."

Sid agreed they should go elsewhere. They moved upward above the forest, and in reference to the earthly globe, eastward out across the Atlantic Ocean. Spreading their spiritual arms and circling silently above the water, each pondered what they had experienced and the questions that remained. Finally aware, first separately, then together, of a realization that all they had learned, all they had believed about life beyond the living was now upended. And they felt joy. Smiling at each other, there was no need to speak or to name the pleasure of shared companionship and discovery. The two spirit friends were simply . . . present.

A voice broke the silence. "Hi guys!"

Kiki and Dave appeared beside them. "You will not believe all that we have seen!" Kiki spoke with bubbly enthusiasm. Dave nodded with peaceful agreement.

"We have a few things to report, as well," responded Sid.

CHAPTER 14

A CALL TO ACTION

Kiki and Dave traded stories with the two older men-spirits, starting with the younger pair's travels around the globe. Kiki in particular burst out a rapid-fire report about seeing sights both novel and wonderful, filling her with curiosity about what next to explore. Dave had to pull her back to task when she went on far too long about why Iceland was named Iceland and Greenland was named Greenland when, in fact, Iceland was much greener than Greenland and Greenland had much more ice than Iceland.

"Whew! Thank you for the interruption," said Kiki, finally able to slow herself sufficiently to allow others to speak. All four wore big smiles at that moment, the others thoroughly entertained by her sense of wonder and excitement.

At length Sid and Ambrose moved to tell Dave the story of his wife's narrow escape from death. He listened carefully as all four spirits continued their float and drift above clouds that broke intermittently to show the blue-green of the sea below them. When Dave seemed to show no discernible reaction to the story, the three other spirits looked at each other, not sure how to proceed. Ambrose spoke in a gentle manner designed to avoid a scolding tone. "I must say, I cannot help but notice your calm and unflappable reception of a most disturbing sequence of events concerning your wife and previous place of residence."

Dave looked at him directly and responded with no indication that he took the question as a rebuke. "I'm surprised, myself, that I'm not more upset, but that other life seems so long ago and, well, I've been told that I shouldn't care about those kinds of things anymore."

Sid and Ambrose glanced at each other, aware that another question threatened to explode from each of them. Ambrose posed the question. "If I may be so bold, and dear man, please know I ask not with scorn but with genuine curiosity, who exactly is it that told you that you should not care?"

Kiki read the confusion on Dave's face and asked, "Why are we all so stuck on this question of how people know what they know and who told us what to think? Nobody ever told me that I shouldn't care. And saying I don't care does not fit me. Okay, sure, I'm putting aside my concern for the life I once had, but we are here now. If we're dead or not dead . . . I don't care about that. But I do care about all of you. And what difference does it make who told what to whom or not?"

Kiki looked first at Ambrose then at Dave. Neither spoke.

Dave continued. "You know, I don't really remember. Kiki didn't ever say that, and it's not like I've met that many other people here . . . not to talk to, I mean. But it seems like something I have been taught, something important."

Sid inserted himself eagerly into the conversation. "Do you mind if we pursue this, my new friend? I and Mr. Bierce here, have had some recent experiences that leave us perplexed. You might have something useful to tell us."

"I'll tell you anything I can," said Dave. "But it's just like I'm remembering something that I was told, but for the life of me I can't remember who told it or when I learned it. Kind of like there's this little voice in my head, in the back of my mind, that says, 'Forget about the life you had. Forget about the people you knew.'"

Kiki stepped in. "That's the same thing as when Mr. Bierce

asked me how I knew certain things about what happened to you, Dave. I knew the story of how you died, but not how I knew it. It's like some things you just know, but you don't know how you know them. Is this making any more sense to you?" She turned to Sid and Ambrose.

The two older men looked at each other and simultaneously spoke, "Maybe." Then they laughed, their giddy heads filling with the nectar of discovery and wonder. It became clear to both of them that they wanted the conversation to continue between just the two of them. They thanked Dave for his information and asked him and Kiki what was next for them.

"We're going to have a big surprise for you before too long," Kiki announced.

Feigning interest in the forthcoming surprise, Ambrose and Sid continued in passable small talk while Kiki and Dave headed back to ground.

Ambrose and Sid continued their soaring trajectory above the open blue ocean, moving in silence, weightless, simultaneously gathering their thoughts for more conversation and basking in pure joy of an evolving discovery.

Finally, Sid opened their dialogue. "I am not wise. I have been twiddling my cosmic thumbs for all this time. I can't believe we . . . I . . . never even considered the possibility of the presence of these beings we can only name as the 'others.' They are so clearly here, beside us in this realm. They have been leading us in a certain direction, to a certain understanding."

Ambrose nodded. "They have been gently guiding us toward disinterest, at least until recently. Leading us away from the toil of care, worry, and concern. You once found it, found your perfect, smiling peace there in that little church. As for myself, what have I been doing but reading and re-reading my modest— if modest not be too glorious a word—modest little words on paper and congratulating myself for my existence?

"But what are they, man? Are they gods, demons, something else entirely? Should we be afraid . . . should we worship them?"

"I feel no pull to worship. I turn toward more complicated measures than what I understand as worship," said Ambrose.

"More complicated? It's complicated beyond understanding already. We don't even know who or what they are or whether to fear or worship them. How?" Sid conveyed a pleading tone in his question.

Ambrose said with conviction, "You are culture-bound, my friend. You need to think anew. You need to make and then fully accept a simple observation, and when you embrace that simple observation, you will see how complicated this really is."

"What observation? Tell me, man! No more riddles!" Sid had fallen back into the role of the supplicant to Ambrose as his mentor.

He held out both hands, palms upward as if offering a feast. "These spirits, whatever we may call them . . . they are changing."

"Changing?"

Ambrose continued while he nodded his head repeatedly and moved his hands in a circular motion as if asking Sid to give him something. "You said it yourself. You believe, as do I, that they have been here in the background for all these centuries that you have been here. You agree that the once human spirits who come here, for short times or long, are guided in a certain way, to . . . no, not *to*, but *through* disinterest."

"Yes. Until now?" Sid's eyes lit up like a rising sun.

"Yes. Until now. Until you called the dogs to Dave's resting place. And I wrestled with Dave's raging and fractured spirit. That was not our doing, our volition. We were at best an instrument. But here is the key: they were not disinterested when we acted on their behalf, or at lease consistent with their intention. They took action! And they seem to be calling us to action."

Ambrose paused, moved closer to Sid, and looked down at his own hands, seemingly formed around an imaginary sphere. He moved his hands further apart, then back together as if forming a circular object, or a thought. "And in the house, when Grove fell to his death and Tom spared Suzanne. It was an action measured for an end!" Ambrose frowned and reflected on the words he just spoke. "Sid, did you hear what I just said?"

"What? Yes . . . but what part—?"

"In the house! I said *in the house!* I think I have been ignoring something right before me! Could the house be what ties all of this together? Things have been upside down since I took up residence in Old Robin. And there is one more thing I have not revealed. The house library holds a large collection of Mr. Bibby's collected books and papers. The material passed down to and through all the subsequent owners. Some of my works were among them!"

"What are you saying, my friend? That Mr. Bibby's spirit still lives here and has some hand in our current adventures?"

Ambrose nodded excitedly. "He could be here in this very house!"

Sid shook his head. "An assumption as yet without evidence, but perhaps no more preposterous than what we have already experienced."

They both fell silent, reflecting on their words.

"Are you afraid?" said Ambrose.

"Should I be? Are you?"

"Perhaps we should be. You know better than I, for you have spent multiples of my time on the journey in this space. Yet in my comparatively brief tenure I did come to have a certain faith in some constancy here. Is it not fair to say that for all the world's ills, that for countless centuries, *events have been matching themselves together in that wondrous mosaic to some parts of which, dimly discernible, we give the name of history*? Are we not now watching, or perhaps even responsible for, a marred harmony of the previous pattern? This is unsettling."[15]

Sid paused, then smiled, and gave his response, "The one pattern or harmony where I always found relief is one of finding myself to be not so important. We are not on trial here. We are the ones receiving, not acting. My friend, we must trust this whatever it is that is happening. The world of the spirits, like the world of man, is unfolding as it must."

Ambrose gave assent with his eyes and spoke no more of fear. "So, I will never again speak of myself as if I were the center of the universe, but there are more subtle things as well. Ever since young Kiki arrived, I have been a changed man. I feel empathy for her and her predicament. Such an emotion from me, a truly heartfelt concern for the trials of others, was rare enough for me in the world of smoke and gravity. It has been even more unusual since I came here to this middle world. But it is unmistakably present. And then there is the biggest thing of all."

"The biggest thing of all? Can you not stop being the purveyor of riddles? Tell me!"

"I am compelled to write." Ambrose smiled again.

---

15 The description of "events matching themselves together" in a mosaic and harmonious pattern appeared in slightly different phraseology in the short story "One of the Missing."

Sid threw up his hands in mock discovery. "Your commentary!"

"Yes, you really need to hear what I wrote. Are you ready?"

Sid laughed. "I stand ready to be convinced that your renewed ability to write is the most glorious outcome of all this. I celebrate the happy truth that the universe exists chiefly, if not exclusively, for your acts of creative self-expression. Indeed, you are who you are, and you are my friend. Tell me now about this commentary."

CHAPTER 15

AMBROSE'S COMMENTARY

Before proceeding with the telling of his commentary, his first literary creation since he left the world of sun and sky to accept his home in the spirit realm, Ambrose asked if they might be able to call forth an audience to hear his performance. Sid pronounced himself in no way surprised by such a request and produced several acquaintances to attend the event. Sid made it clear that he did not know them very well and did not call them friends in the way he valued Ambrose.

One of those who agreed to attend was the young priest from the Episcopal Church who had died his earthly death soon after qualifying for his role and robes, struck down by a random blood malignancy. Father Robert, his church name, shared a part of the Episcopal Church near Sid but spent most of his time lurking about the religious ornamentation of the church building, peering out the stained-glass windows. He once confessed to Sid, in a rare conversation, that his soul churned with doubt and mistrust about what lay beyond, unable to gather sufficient faith to move on to the other side.

The second of Sid's three invitees, a former mayor of a midsized northeastern US city, carried the taint of a lifetime of graft and fraud. When approaching his mortal demise, he tried a deathbed confession and repentance that felt awkward to all those around him. His plea for mercy and forgiveness did not seem genuine or prove rewarding even to the supplicant himself. The man knew his heart was not sincere and he assumed it was not a successful entreaty to whomever should pass judgement on such things and determine his fate beyond his days of eagerly embracing all of the seven deadly sins.

Jewish by birth, but a converted Christian, the aspiring politician had chosen his faith to appeal to his constituency, even changing his last name to name to Andrews. Now with no more election campaigns, he felt genuinely lost. His greatest fear was that there might really be Hell and that he could be judged deserving of it. Had anyone been measuring his stay in the spirit world by human years, the seventy-fifth anniversary of his arrival in his current spirit world lay just ahead.

Kiki and Dave delivered, in part, on their promised surprise when they arrived at Ambrose's event with a crowd of close to fifty in number. All joined Ambrose in the general vicinity of a grassy hillside, just outside of Richmond, Virginia. Being spirits, they did not exactly sit on the cool, green grass, but they gathered around in their chosen state of repose or attentive posture and waited quietly for Ambrose to begin his presentation.

Both Sid and Ambrose were sufficiently curious about Kiki and Dave's multitude that they begged an explanation. Kiki did the talking, "Well, you see, it's like this. Dave and I both came to the same realization that it was great to zoom around the planet and see all these places—my God, the Grand Canyon was incredible—but after a while we got a little bored. And Dave especially, since he hasn't met and talked to a lot of people—as spirits, I mean. So, we came up with the idea that we would look for more company, the way you introduced us to Victoria."

Sid opened his arms and gestured toward the crowd. "You have a small multitude gathered in one group. One generally does not see so many together like that."

"Well, we sort of gathered them up," answered Kiki. "We

asked ourselves where you would go to meet new spirits. And Dave, he says, maybe hospitals and old folks' homes, that's where a lot of people, you know, die, if you know what I mean."

Ambrose and Sid glanced at each other with a look that acknowledged they had just been taught the obvious, but until now had never thought of it quite in that way.

Dave joined the conversation. "All of these people are recently dead, within a week or maybe two. It's not all the people who died in a week in all of Richmond's hospitals and nursing homes, but it's the ones who seemed to be curious about us, and each other, where they are now and all that."

Ambrose took a moment to survey the crowd and reflect upon the collection of people. A solid majority were elderly, mostly women, but several children under ten held tight to the hand of one or another of the adults, looking shy but not afraid. One man still dressed as a firefighter stood off from the group. Two young women in workout clothes kept mostly to themselves, positioned a clear and separate distance behind the main gathering.

Kiki beamed with pride. "We've kind of, like, been having a class for everybody. They have so many questions. It's like what you guys did for me when I came here. I think they think it's really great to hear somebody's experience, even if no one has all the answers."

"So, why did Sid ask us to come here now?" said Dave. "He said something like you were going to tell a story or something like that and you wanted lots of people here. Is there more to it than that?"

Before anyone could respond to Dave's entreaty, one more guest arrived: Victoria Vandupont. She seemed to appear out of nowhere, presenting herself in her dramatic manner with a look of expectation that begged the attention of any and all. Most of the gathering turned to her but no one spoke, so she did.

"Well, you all look like you are surprised to find me here. But why would you think that I would miss a *live* show? Despite Mr. Bierce's characteristic and withering negativity, this has the promise of being entertaining." Victoria moved to the side of Father Robert. "I will stand here with this handsome and gracious young man and will look forward to his critique of what we are about to hear."

Father Robert himself did not seem surprised at Victoria's attaching herself to him. His smile conveyed a welcome consent.

Sid took Victoria's pronouncement as his cue to ready the crowd with an introduction of today's event and the general nature of the performance. Sid gave a flattering description of Ambrose's accomplishments in life without revealing the details of what he was about to deliver.

Sid gestured with open arms to the assembled spirits. "Here in the spirit world, we do not create. We seem to lack the capability to create art, or music, or poetry . . . that is, until now. Somehow, our speaker today has managed to harness this fire we call creativity. Ladies and gentlemen, I give you Mr. Ambrose Bierce." He turned and bowed to Ambrose.

Positioned further up the hill above the small crowd that came to hear him, Ambrose looked down and saw faces that were equal measure of sad and puzzled, but respectfully awaiting his words. He began without hesitation.

"Some of you know my book called the *Devil's Dictionary*. In it I give my take on the word 'obsession.' In doing so, in my book, I invoke the memory of the Gadarene swine. Today I will tell you more about this story that is found in the Christian Gospels. I expect that it is a story well known to some here, but you need not have been familiar with the story beforehand. I will tell all of it that you need to know.

"During his ministry, during his life upon the earth, Jesus traveled to the Gadarene islands where he visited a small village. In that place he encountered a troubled man. The Bible tells us this man was possessed by demons. He lived as a wild man among the tombs. He could not be contained by men even with the use of chains. Yet despite his unfortunate situation he and the people of the town seemed to have found a way to live beside one another, as long as he kept his distance. There he wandered from place to place, living mostly among the tombs of the dead, a tortured soul if ever one drew breath, crying out and cutting himself with sharp stones.

"Now when Jesus stepped from his boat, the man immediately ran to Jesus. And the accounts from the Gospels of Matthew and Luke differ a little in what actually happened next, but it is clear that Jesus recognized there were demons who had taken possession of the man. Jesus then spoke to the spirits, commanding them to confess their name. 'My name is Legion,' the demons replied, for there were many, many demons inside him."

As Ambrose spoke, Sid was figuratively bouncing up and down in his virtual seat, as if wanting to raise his hand and give some sort of comment or ask a question. But Ambrose was not conducting an interactive event and thus continued without acknowledgement of Sid's enthusiasm. His voice rose to a higher level of urgency. He gestured dramatically. Ambrose was filled with pride that he seemed to be capturing an audience.

"At this point the demons became terrified of the power of Jesus. They anticipated their own destruction. They pleaded with him and begged for his mercy. And Jesus took pity on them and did not annihilate them. He simply moved them out of the man and into a herd of swine. After this transfer of the demons, the man sat still, calm, free from the effects of possession by the demons."

After a brief dramatic pause, offered in order for the audience to appreciate the event as it unfolded so far, Ambrose continued. "But unfortunately, the swine now held within them the fearful demons and they were terrified. They ran wildly in desperation of their plight. Careening down a hill, they fell into a pond of water and drowned."

Another dramatic pause. "What transpired next is the moment of illumination. The people of the town came running toward Jesus. They were equal parts angry and afraid. They were angry over losing their herd of swine. This was a great catastrophe! They were afraid because of the manifested power of this stranger among them. Their anger prevailed, and they demanded that Jesus restore their loss and then immediately depart."

By this time Ambrose noticed that he had the true attention of all of his audience. "So, what is the lesson here? What does all this mean?" He turned his head dramatically from right to left in a wide scan of the crowd.

Sid's politician friend burst out laughing, then covered his face, stifling a full measure fit of laughter. He refused to say why this so amused him.

A small woman near the front, one who had obviously been blessed with a very long life, spoke up and said, "I know what you're getting at, mister. Want me to say it?"

Ambrose smiled and gestured with open hand, "I do want you to say it, my dear lady."

She straightened her posture, looked to the right, then the left and spoke, "It means that most people, when asked to make a choice between Savior and swine . . . they will choose swine."

Several in the crowd laughed. The politician again laughed so hard he snorted but still refused to name the construct of his delight. He pointed at Ambrose with both index fingers and begged Ambrose, "Go ahead and say it. We both know what you're going to say."

"Yes, here it is," said Ambrose. "The fact remains that people will never give up enough of their own pork to care for the needs of the most vulnerable among us."

Raucous laughter ensued from the politician, coming in spurts so hard he cried, but through his outburst managed to say, "It's just good old pork barrel politics as usual!" Clearly pleased with himself, he continued a sustained burst of laughter with an intensity beyond anyone else in the crowd, calling unashamed attention to himself.

"Well done, my friend! Well done!" trumpeted Sid, prompting the crowd for applause. All made the motion of clapping with their hands despite the absence of sound due to the want of solid matter striking solid matter. Ambrose stood tall, his hands clasped behind his back, his head turned slightly upward and eyes closed, clearly glowing in the approval.

Sid moved closer to Ambrose, speaking discreetly for his ears only. "You do know, my creative friend, that your first writing is on the theme of compassion, or more specifically, the lack of compassion in the hearts of men?"

Ambrose gave him a quick glance and returned to bask further in the glow of acclaim from the crowd.

Soon the crowd began to move away, circling around the side of the hill slowly. Kiki approached Ambrose and Sid, and waited while Ambrose absorbed a sufficient measure of

approval and congratulations. Having garnered their attention, she said, "I guess this is goodbye, for now at least."

Neither Sid nor Ambrose understood the significance of her
words. Sid asked, "So, where are you off to now?"

Kiki paused, smiled, and said softly, "We are going to leave
this world now. We're going to move on . . . to cross over to the
other side."

CHAPTER 16

DEPARTURES

Ambrose was twice surprised by Kiki's revelation that she would now move beyond this middle spirit world to whatever lay beyond. The first surprise was that she had made the decision to do so; the second surprise came when he felt her revelation tear at his heart, or wherever it is that feelings of loss and regret attack the spirit form. He could not manage to deliver to her the gift of saying, "I don't want you to go; I will miss you," but he did ask her to explain.

"So, it's really rather simple," she answered. "I've pretty much used up my energy and interest here and I've figured out that there's only a few possibilities for what could be waiting for me in the next world. And I'm ready, whatever it is."

Ambrose did feel the personal bite of Kiki's statement that there was little in this current world that interested her—not even him, or the things that he once wrote, or might now write—but he kept silent and allowed her to continue.

"And part of it is that in these classes we've been having— that's what I call them, 'classes'—with these other people we've met . . . there's this one lady who's just totally convinced there is a heaven over there. She talks about looking forward to seeing her parents and her brothers and sisters again and she's just so ready to go."

"She could be right," Sid allowed, endorsing neither faith nor doubt.

Kiki ignored his comment. "So, here's my take. I guess there are three things that could be waiting for me. One, there's a heaven, and if that's the case I think I'll get in. I was not a bad person. I could have gone to church more, but whatever. Two, we all get loaded up and sent back for reincarnation, and that ain't such a bad thing to think about?" She lifted her voice at the end of her statement, making it into a question that she clearly posed to Sid and Ambrose. She paused, making it clear she wanted a reply.

Ambrose remembered sharing his fear about the possibility of another earthly episode for him but chose to not repeat himself. Instead, he offered a gentle statement that he intended as one of hope for her, if indeed she was given another chance at an earthly life. "I wish for you a better life than the one you currently hold memory for."

Kiki responded with passion. "Well, thank you very much, Mr. Ambrose Bierce, but I know what you're thinking. You're thinking that I didn't have such a bad life and that I could be making a big mistake. But I don't care. I want another chance and I'll take that chance. If I end up burned up from a bomb falling on my house, or beat to death by a no-good husband, or even if I come back in some hellish place and starve to death or drown in a mudslide, I'll take that chance! Because I just might find someone who will love the hell out of me and I just might have five kids who grow up happy and strong, so I'll take that chance, Mr. Ambrose Bierce! I want a chance to love and feel and connect to the people I missed out on because I was so young and stupid and didn't have a clue what life was really about. So there!"

Hands on her hips, she looked him in his spiritual eyes.

Some amount of time passed as Kiki, Ambrose, and Sid looked silently at each other for what might have been just a mortal second, but within the possibilities of their current world, even that measure of time allowed each of them unlimited and unbound reflection upon their shared experience with each other. They bathed in the pleasure of true connectedness. Had they human form and substance, they would have clung each to the others, cried, and reveled in fond embrace. Bound by the limits of their present realm, however, they gratefully accepted the rewards of spiritual companionship available to them. "And there's another thing for me," said Dave. "I went by my old house the other day and I saw that real estate guy and my wife having coffee together. They've clearly got a friendship and who-knows-what-else going on between them. Not my concern, and I don't really care, but there's nothing here for me. So, I'll be going with Kiki. I'll take my chances too."

The four then became aware that the crowd stood near, clearly observing them. Those people who Dave and Kiki had gathered looked expectantly toward them. Before Kiki could redirect her attention to them, Sid asked her a final question. "You said there were three possibilities for the life beyond this one. What's the third?"

Kiki smiled at Sid and replied, "Maybe some version of what you talk so much about. A total freedom from desire. Maybe just a really, really, really quiet place. Maybe even, just . . . just nothing."

"I hope not," offered Sid.

"Me neither," responded Kiki. "But I do have one more question for you, Mr. Sid, or whatever your real name is. I still don't totally get that baseball, time, and Buddhism thing, but one thing you said really stuck with me. That thing about finding time in a teacup."

A smile, large and radiant, now graced Sid's face as he replied, "Ah. Oh yes. Oh yes. I will confess I stole that image, and changed it around a little, from a poem about God I once heard. It is a poem whose creator is lost to history but has remained in my mind all this time. Would you like to hear it? I think it may be illustrative at this moment."

Kiki nodded enthusiastically and Sid recited his poem.

I once found God in a teacup, and the people got really mad.
They came running, and put their hands on me and held me
*   down.*
They're letting me go now, I'm still afraid but not hurt.
Come get me, and lift me up on your big shoulders, and take
*   me home.*

Kiki looked at Sid with a puzzled expression. "Well, that's very interesting but I can't say I for sure know what it means. You say it is supposed to tell me something?"

Sid replied softly, "Yes, but it has meaning only if I am right about our next life, that we indeed do have that future life that awaits us. I believe we do have that life. But the message of the poem is that we must be careful about where we say that we find God. Some people are quite severe about where they allow God to be found."

Kiki gave an understanding smile.

At that moment, all present felt an overwhelming spiritual pull coming from something or somewhere not understood by any of them. Sid and Ambrose sensed one version of it, but they were drawn away in a direction different from the other spirits, and moved a short distance away from the crowd. Ambrose felt overwhelmed by all that was happening. He sensed he was losing control of his ability to think and to speak. He experienced profound sadness, and fear, and something else. He searched his mind for words to describe it. Nothing came. He wondered if those he called the others were trying to communicate something to him.

Kiki, Dave, and their fifty new friends moved further away,

their attention captured by that unknown beyond. Father Robert moved into the middle of the group, smiled into the faces of several of them, and reached out as if to hold hands with an older woman spirit who beamed a smile back to him. Then he moved away from them, separating himself from the departing spirits, clearly not ready to go with them. Victoria, too, joined him, moving away from those leaving.

The laughing politician stood in the center of the crowd. He inserted himself between the two young women in jogging clothes, one on either side, a huge smile on his face. He made eye contact with Ambrose and silently mouthed the words "Why not?" The two women wiped their eyes as if real tears had flowed from their current composition, but they seemed comforted by the laughing man's proximity and appeared to be more peaceful and relaxed.

Kiki turned back to Ambrose and Sid. "I have one more big surprise for you before I go. I bet it's something you're going to think about for a while."

Ambrose struggled to control his emotions and organize his thoughts. He looked directly at Kiki, who was moving to her left and gesturing with her palms as if revealing or introducing someone to him. Then it became clear. Emerging from the anonymity of the crowd was Tom. Tom the thief. Tom the accomplice to murder. Tom who had spared Suzanne's life by cutting her bonds. Dave stood beside him, his hand positioned as if resting supportively on his shoulder.

Some of the people began to sing; some began to pray. They were now ready to go . . . somewhere. Gradually rising into the air, those leaving grew smaller and less distinct. The group moved closer to each other. Eventually they coalesced into a single point, all together in a single small and shrinking space. And then they were gone.

Following the departure of Kiki, Dave, and the rest of the group, Ambrose and Sid stood apart, thinking they were alone. Together and individually, for just a moment, or for half an earth-measured lifetime, they tried to comprehend and accept what had just taken place. Then they heard voices behind them. Turning, they discovered Victoria and Father Robert, facing each other in prayer pose.

After waiting patiently for Victoria and Father Robert to finish their prayers, Sid and Ambrose approached the couple. Taking the lead, Sid fumbled out a question. "Victoria, may I speak with you? I need to know something and I think only you can tell me."

"Well, of course," said Victoria with a smile. "But why do you think you must ask permission? Is that why you have never addressed me before? Was I unworthy of the attention from an exalted one?"

Victoria's reply rang true to Ambrose. He had criticized Sid before because he never actually approached her in a respectful, or even in a passingly polite or social way. Sid had confessed that he felt little interest in her. He once told Ambrose that Victoria might be someone to study, observe, and wonder about but not engage as an equal. Sid now turned to Ambrose for help.

"Even the most capable have their blind spots," said Ambrose. "But we both have been unsure if you held us truly welcome in your life."

"Okay, that's good," said Victoria. "I can see you both are trying to approach this with some humility. Nevertheless, I know what your question is. But I'm sorry, I am going to make you ask it." She looked directly at Sid and waited, hands in folded position in front of her, face lifted expectantly and serene.

"Victoria, we have observed you," said Sid, "and we have learned from others, that somehow you have found a special bond with a living person, Presiding Bishop Gerald. How have you done this? I have been in the spirit world for many times greater than the years you have spent here. I have never seen or heard others speak of the ability to actually engage in ordered conversation with the living."

Victoria looked down, seemingly lost in her own thoughts. Sid and Ambrose, along with Father Robert, waited with apparent patience, but Sid and Ambrose held their words.

"I'm afraid you are going to find some discomfort in what I have to say," she told them rebukingly. "There is no way this can be said without hurting your feelings. But that can't be helped. You have not seen this ability to communicate between worlds because you have not been willing to look for it. Conversations like mine with Bishop Gerald happen all the time."

Ambrose felt a combination of shock, disbelief, and embarrassment. He saw a reaction on Sid's face that could only have been the same. If what Victoria said were true, they must have been blind in some fundamental way about their spirit world.

Victoria continued. "Mr. Sid—I guess it's okay to address you in that way, but during the time we have been in close proximity, you have never actually told me directly what is your true name, or how to address you, so that's the best I can do. The Bishop tells me that you are considered by many to be uniquely wise. But here is what I think. You approach the world with primarily your head and less with your heart, although you do seem to try. As for you, Mr. Bierce, you start with your head and then filter all things through your gut, and you, too, miss your heart on the way down."

Ambrose was astonished that Victoria would address them in this way. He could tell Sid felt the same. It was Sid who gave the first reply. "Thank you for this. I needed to hear all that you have said. Your wisdom far surpasses my own."

Ambrose lowered his head in humility. "I hope you will grant that we are asking you with genuine respect and are not dismissive of what you say, but how have we missed this?"

"I'm not sure if it's because your hearts were broken when you were alive or because your hearts were not broken. I only know that I died with a broken heart and I came here in such pain. During my earthly life I married and lived with the best man who ever walked the planet. He walked away from the opportunity to enrich himself with money by crushing others, and when he refused and did walk away from that, there were people who crushed him and we died penniless. I myself could have managed that, but to see him broken like that, my heart shattered. Somehow Bishop Gerald found me here with my broken heart, and we have talked of this time and again."

Ambrose felt his mind race with questions but no coherent thought presented. Keeping silent appeared to be the best decision.

"So now I'll let you off the hook a little," she said. "There is a practical reason you never saw anything like my communion with Bishop Gerald. That kind of conversation usually leads to a quick passage out of this version of the afterlife. You do know there is something beyond here, don't you?"

Sid and Ambrose both smiled and nodded meekly, unconvincingly.

"So, let me tell you more about me. My husband died a decade before me. Bishop Gerald helped him move along quickly, with help from other spirits already here. The Bishop also promised my husband he would look out for me, that he would find me when it was my turn. He reached into this world, found me to be lost and confused, and he restored me to hope and peace. I asked how I could repay him. He gave me a job to do."

"So, you have been staying here for some purpose?" Ambrose asked. "We simply thought that you were stuck here, in a form of spiritual paralysis."

"Yes, you 'simply thought,' as you put it. A better way might be that you 'thought simply.'"

Ambrose opened and lifted his hands. "May we ask what job you were given to do?"

Victoria turned to Father Robert with raised eyebrows. "May we tell them?"

Father Robert frowned and looked away, not quite hiding his sadness and pain, then looked back at the others and spoke, "I am her job. Bishop Gerald has set her upon me as a hound of heaven. She pursues me relentlessly to tell me that I should not fear—"

"You don't have to tell them anything more, Father Robert," interrupted Victoria.

"Then I'll end with this," Father Robert added. "I sometimes did terrible things to those who once trusted me. I believe that hell's fire waits for me. Perhaps this is not so. When I can give up this fear, Victoria's work will be done, and we will move on together."

"Dear people," Ambrose stumbled, "please accept this truly foolish question. Victoria, have you gained insight, or any glimpse of what lies beyond this life?"

Her exasperation in full show, she answered. "Of course not. What or who do you think I am? No one knows. But I believe what Bishop Gerald believes, that with faith, hope, and an open heart, something good waits. Something good waits for Father Robert."

"We are both waiting for Bishop Gerald," said Father Robert. "He is a very old mortal man. He is ill. He will be joining us here soon. Victoria says he carries directly to me a message. For some reason I am not capable of hearing him or talking with him the way that Victoria can. He must deliver the message to me when he comes here. It is the message that I can be forgiven. If that is true, if he does that, then I will believe. Then we will move along together, the three of us, and any others who wish to join us. I do not yet have faith, or I should say what faith I once had is lost, but I have hope, and I had none of that until Victoria."

Victoria then gathered Father Robert to her side and they moved away. She looked back over her shoulder and said, "We'll be going back to the church now. We often sit there together and wait."

Victoria turned to leave, then put her hand to her cheek and exclaimed, "Dear me! Now I am the one who is thoughtless! I forgot an important message. Mr. Bierce, you must come back to the church when it is convenient. A letter has arrived for you."

Ambrose and Sid spoke simultaneously and with equal measure of surprise.

"A letter?"

CHAPTER 17

A LETTER FOR AMBROSE

After sputtering incoherently for a time sufficient for a mortal minute of comprehensible speech, Ambrose managed to give verbal form to actual questions. "A physical letter? In an envelope? From whom? Was there a return address?"

Victoria answered his questions parsimoniously. "Why, yes. It is a standard kind of letter in what one would call a business-sized envelope. Your name was written in the appropriate place and manner, in a lovely cursive script, and appears to have been written with a quill pen."

Victoria showed some obvious pleasure that Ambrose was stunned speechless. His mouth opened and closed without sound. She continued speaking slowly, clearly enjoying this interaction. "Black ink. There was no return address. There was no postage stamp. My understanding is that it was found in the church mailbox among the more usual collection of bills and advertising flyers."

Ambrose's face looked like that of a frustrated child. "How am I to open such a thing, having no corporeal hands?"

"That has all been taken into consideration. There is no problem. The letter was retrieved from the usual fare by the Bishop himself. Since he already knows all about you from me, he opened the letter and has it open for display on a corner table in my room. It is a single page."

"Did you read it? What did it say?"

Victoria replied with dramatic mock offense, "Certainly not!

I do not read the personal mail of others. That would be such a betrayal of all manners and customs by which I have lived my modest life. I may have lost the trappings of a certain class of people, but I have not lost my integrity." Victoria completed her retort with a calm grace, obviously not surprised by the question.

"I must go there without delay," said Ambrose.

"And I shall accompany you," said Sid.

"No. This is something I must do—"

"Mr. Bierce!" Sid exploded. "I know what you are thinking. You think it's from the others. And I stand ready to acknowledge that somehow you are some kind of chosen one to receive this communication and perhaps knowledge and, indeed, even have experiences from some unknown and perhaps wonderful power or place. But will you really deny your friend the privilege of bearing witness to this? Am I not your friend? Are you not mine?"

Ambrose grew silent, then looked at Sid and said, "Of course you are right. I need to calm myself. I am in too much of a hurry to rush off to this . . . this . . . mystery. Of course, it is from the others. Who else would know that I am here in this place and time, if there still is such a thing as time? And I am your friend and you are mine. We shall go together."

Sid and Ambrose entered the Bishop's office, also Victoria's room, and immediately saw the letter on a table in a corner opposite Victoria's television. On the way there they had exhausted speculation about what the letter could contain, yet were able to agree to a point of certainty that it was a communication from the mysterious others who shared the spirit world with them. Ambrose wondered out loud whether this was leading to his end-of-life in the spirit world, or as he put it, "the fate of my soul." Sid did not express an opinion about that theory and kept silent any feeling that Ambrose was once again making himself the center of the universe.

Finally, they stood over the letter, weighed open by a Bible at the top and a hymnal at the bottom. The entirety of the letter was four words. No greeting. No salutation. No signature.

Attend to your nature

Ambrose felt bewildered beyond expression. Disappointment flowed through both men. When they were at length able to discuss what they read, they came to a quick agreement that they should not have expected anything other than continuing mystery.

Ambrose added, "Of course, that's the thinking part of this, but this is also personal. I have been given a task. I must 'attend to my nature,' and yet I have no idea how to proceed. What is my nature? Are they talking about the nature of man? Or is it uniquely me, and my nature to which they issue a challenge? Is this an indictment? Should I confess, pray, and fall to the ground and grovel? And what does the word 'attend' mean here? Is there some action I should take? I am lost."

The two friends talked as the clock on the wall in the Bishop's office marked the passing of earthly time. They did not count or care about the many cycles that passed on the mechanical device. Their conversation rose and fell, grew silent, then explosive, but in the end, Sid added little more to the dialogue than to help Ambrose repeat questions about the letter and the challenge contained within. Sid looked at Ambrose with his characteristic peaceful smile and said, "My dear friend . . . everything is new."

As the men again renewed their conversation, Victoria appeared at the door, and the sound of the church filling up with parishioners drew the men out of their preoccupation.

Victoria spoke. "It is time for the Bishop's funeral service. He died yesterday. I would be honored if you two wonderful men would attend the service with me."

Ambrose felt some relief to have their deliberations interrupted. He eagerly assented to Victoria's request and together the trio positioned themselves at the back of the church above the living parishioners. A large choir of experienced singers had already taken their places and began a hymn that Victoria said was the Bishop's personal favorite, "For the Beauty of the Earth." She added that the hymn spoke personally to her. Ambrose noted the look of obvious pleasure in her countenance as the song commenced.

Victoria closed her eyes and seemed to escape to a place and time of her own peaceful creation, in a moment uniquely hers. Ambrose, too, responded to the song, but in a very different way. Victoria and Ambrose entered into and held tightly to their own disparate thoughts, alone in their inner worlds as the song burst gloriously forth from the grand pipe organ and carried aloft by sixty angelic voices of the choir.

The choir sang: "For the beauty of the earth, for the beauty of the skies."

Ambrose heard the music but his thoughts turned to those of a small boy of about six years of age. This boy was the son of a planter who had once been a soldier who had served gallantly, following his country's flag against naked savages to tame a restless new land. The soldier-father gave up war and returned to family, but once such warrior-fire is kindled it is never extinguished, and through books and tales he passed certain passions to a son. This small boy took up his father's passion and made a wooden sword, and in his daily play marched against imaginary foes, victorious always.[16]

The choir continued: "For the love which from our birth over and around us lies."

Victoria spoke softly to Ambrose about her love for the Bishop and her hope for reunion with her beloved husband, but his attention was not given to her.

Ambrose's thoughts stayed with the boy, who *made reckless by the ease with which he overcame invisible foes attempting to stay his advance, the small boy with wooden sword committed the common enough military error of pushing the pursuit to a dangerous extreme, until he found himself upon the margin of a wide but shallow brook, whose rapid waters barred his direct advance against the flying foe that had crossed with illogical ease. But the intrepid victor was not to be baffled; the spirit of the race which had passed the great sea burned* inside the boy and would not be put out. He moved further into the breach.[17]

The chorus filled the church with glorious song: "For the beauty of each hour of the day and of the night."

Victoria moved her lips with silent song, her face serene. She spoke to Ambrose of a time when she was loved by a strong man and her world was filled with priceless treasures and caring friends. Ambrose stared with half-closed eyes, his face fixed with sorrowful expression, his heart and mind back with the boy of his memory.

Advancing from the bank of the creek the brave but foolish young warrior suddenly found himself confronted with a new and

---

16 This paragraph consists of slightly altered appropriations or direct quotes of Bierce's work from the short story "Chickamaugua."

17 Ibid.

more formidable enemy: in the path that he was following, sat, bolt upright, with ears erect and paws suspended before it, a rabbit! With a startled cry the child turned and fled, he knew not in what direction, calling with inarticulate cries for his mother, weeping, stumbling, his tender skin cruelly torn by brambles, his little heart beating hard with terror—breathless, blind with tears—lost in the forest! Then, for more than an hour, he wandered with erring feet through the tangled undergrowth, till at last, overcome by fatigue, he lay down in a narrow space between two rocks, within a few yards of the stream and still grasping his toy sword, no longer a weapon but a companion, sobbed himself to sleep.[18]

A soloist took up the hymn. "Hill and vale, and tree and flower, sun and moon and stars of light."

Victoria remembered vacations with family and friends, picnics, and days of endless summers.

Ambrose heard nothing of the Bishop's tribute. The song did not reach him. He was fully with the boy now and this other adventure.

Hours passed, and then the little sleeper rose to his feet. The chill of the evening was in his limbs, the fear of the gloom in his heart. But he had rested, and he no longer wept. With some blind instinct which impelled to action he struggled through the undergrowth about him and came to a more open ground—on his right the brook, to the left a gentle acclivity studded with infrequent trees; over all, the gathering gloom of twilight. A thin, ghostly mist rose along the water. It frightened and repelled him; instead of recrossing, in the direction whence he had come, he turned his back upon it, and went forward toward the dark inclosing wood. Suddenly he saw before him a strange moving object which he took to be some large animal—a dog, a pig— he could not name it; perhaps it was a bear.[19]

---

18 Ibid.
19 Ibid.

The song grew to a magnificent swell, ever higher, "For the joy of human love, brother, sister, parent child."

The sensation of a single tear formed in the corner of Victoria's eye. She blinked it away with a smile. No congregational voice held silent. No congregational soul was left untouched by the music and the moment. The Bishop was truly loved and loving. The people would sing their love with this song that would bring both tears and joy. Ambrose alone was unmoved.

They were men. They crept upon their hands and knees. Some used their hands only, dragging their legs. Some used their knees only, their arms hanging idle at their sides. They strove to rise to their feet, but fell prone in the attempt. They did nothing naturally, and nothing alike, save only to advance foot by foot in the same direction. Singly, in pairs and in little groups, they came on through the gloom, some halting now and again while others crept slowly past them, then resuming their movement. They came by dozens and by hundreds; as far on either hand as one could see in the deepening gloom they extended and the black wood behind them appeared to be inexhaustible.[20]

The music soared on pipe and voice: "Friends on earth and friends above, pleasures pure and undefiled."

Victoria's spirit wept and she wiped her spiritual tears with a small, white cloth with lace border, as if she had been restored to mortal function. She wept for losses. She wept for hope.

Ambrose, unaware of Victoria or the concerns of the congregation, silently embraced pain and terror.

The boy-warrior now *approached one of these crawling figures from behind and with an agile movement mounted it astride. The man sank upon his breast, recovered, flung the small boy fiercely to the ground as an unbroken colt might have done, then turned upon him*

---

20 Ibid.

a face that lacked a lower jaw—from the upper teeth to the throat was a great red gap fringed with hanging shreds of flesh and splinters of bone. The unnatural prominence of nose, the absence of chin, the fierce eyes, gave this man the appearance of a great bird of prey crimsoned in throat and breast by the blood of its quarry. The man rose to his knees, the child to his feet. The man shook his fist at the child; the child, terrified at last, ran to a tree nearby, got upon the farther side of it and took a more serious view of the situation.[21]

Led on by the music, a procession of mourners filed slowly past the Bishop's open coffin. And on they sang, "For each perfect gift of thine, to our race so freely given."

Victoria remained at the back of the church, not needing to join a procession of the living. Her relationship with the Bishop was now changing, but not ending. There was no reason to say goodbye. Ambrose did not mark the movements of the mortals.

The boy turned and ran, unsure of his path, but putting the men behind him. *Confident of the fidelity of his forces, he now entered the belt of woods, passed through it easily in the red illumination, climbed a fence, ran across a field, turning now and again to coquet with his responsive shadow, and so approached the blazing ruin of a dwelling. Desolation everywhere! In all the wide glare not a living thing was visible. He cared nothing for that; the spectacle pleased, and he danced with glee in imitation of the wavering flames. He ran about, collecting fuel, but every object that he found was too heavy for him to cast in from the distance to which the heat limited his approach. In despair he flung in his sword—a surrender to the superior forces of nature. His military career was at an end.*[22]

Shifting his position, his eyes fell upon some outbuildings which had an oddly familiar appearance, as if he had dreamed of them. He stood considering them with wonder, when suddenly the entire

---

21 Ibid.

22 Ibid.

plantation, with its inclosing forest, seemed to turn as if upon a pivot. His little world swung half around; the points of the compass were reversed. He recognized the blazing building as his own home![23]

The grand organ raced toward its triumphant final chord. With one final refrain of transcendent song, the choir and congregation were lifted to share the company of the divine, "Lord of all to thee we raise, this our hymn of grateful praise."

Ambrose concluded his remembering. He returned to what passed as the present. He reflected upon the nature of man, and of his own.

---

23 Ibid.

CHAPTER 18

THE SEARCH GOES ON

Sid joined Ambrose in the space that mankind named as the sky. They moved side by side, viewing the world from high above the clouds. Highways for motorcars appeared as small but distinct lines. Houses of the living randomly dotted the landscape, looking like tiny boxes. The countryside below reached out to the horizon weaving a green, brown, and golden quilt below.

Ambrose asked, "What season is it upon the earth, my friend?"

"Autumn, I suppose. Observe the red tint along the yellow edge of the forest. I think those are maple trees."

"What measure of earthly time has been marked since Dave and Kiki left?"

Sid replied wistfully, "I cannot say. Perhaps a very long time. I know so little."

"You know so much more about this world than do I," said Ambrose. "But I have been aware of a great amount of time passing and a great feeling of separateness, and yes, self-imposed. I once counted this capacity as a strength. I tell myself that I have been here making myself available, waiting for opportunities, but no opportunities present themselves. No peace. No understanding. But as to your other question, I do not have a considered or measured sense of time about this. Perhaps, with no others around, I do not exist. Or perhaps time does not exist unless we are counting it openly."

"Talk in riddles if you will, but I know what you've been doing. You have been waiting for those beings that you call the others to come to you, or call to you? Have you heard nothing?"

A sense of defeat and hopelessness came through in Ambrose's reply. "I have heard nothing. And a sad possibility presents itself to me. I am approaching the idea that perhaps none of this is real."

"Unreal in what manner, man? I promise you I stand—uh . . . float—here, as do you. We think, therefore we—"

"Unreal, in that all of this is merely the last dying thoughts of a fool. That in any real measure of time, I lie dying upon the ground or bed, and that all I had experienced in the world of man and beast is poured out whole, a last pitiful discharge of my brain, all that I have ever learned and experienced, spit out on the ground in one final spilling of life. And as soon as I begin to rot, all of this will vanish."

Sid looked at Ambrose with astonishment. "So, all of my experiences, my existence here, and all that you and I have shared is simply your death seizure? Well, I can't say I'm surprised to hear that. You have an endless capacity to see yourself as the center of all existence. And while that has not made me less fond of you, I reject it. Please, my friend, think more broadly about all you have seen and learned here in the rich and abundant spirit world."

Ambrose held up his hands and shook his head. "Again, I bow to your wisdom. But help me think about this. If you are anything that deserves the name of friend, companion, or fellow traveler, or with any kindness of affiliation, you must engage with me on this. I remember you once burned with curiosity, with an ache to know the identity of this something or someone who is clearly here but shrouded in mystery. Now it is I who cannot turn away from the question. Who are these others and what is their intention?"

Sid proceeded eagerly. "Recall, if you will, two things about our shared wondering in the past. First, are they gods, these others?" Ambrose nodded a confirmation of this recollection, and Sid continued. "We were wrong to see them as omniscient, omnipotent beings. They do have great powers, such as they showed in the borrowing of your memory to do heroic works back in Dave's house. They may have been guiding, or complicating, or somehow involved in the lives of humans for all time. In some cultures, they may fit, they may be accepted, as some kind of imperfect god. To some, gods are well known to have flaws and vulnerabilities."

Ambrose nodded enthusiastically. "So, they are not gods in the way that the Western man thinks of his perfect and all-powerful God. I understand that. My recent communion with them, limited and puzzling as it was, clearly fell short of my view of such a godlike nature. What is the second thing you wish me to recall from our earlier conversations?"

"You quite rightly pointed out there seemed to be a change in their behavior, or their nature, or some sort of change from disinterest to a kind of benevolent investment in a human outcome. We saw it yet did not understand it, but you named it. You discerned that this was a change, and for that I—we—salute you!"

"Go on," instructed Ambrose.

"Do you believe in evolution?"

"Evolution? A science more dismal than economics, but I dare say there is evidence that man is now more than he once was, and may one day be more than he now is. If that is the true nature of your question, yes, I believe in evolution."

Sid lifted a single finger to the sky. "Good. Then here is one possibility. Just as the human changes, a similar process may be unfolding within the spirit world, within these very spirits we seek to encounter and understand."

"What process? What beings? Count me as an ape in measured wisdom and understanding. I cannot see the big picture."

"Okay. First accept the fact that here within the spirit world there are beings who are not and who never were in human form, and accept the fact that they have great and unusual powers not held by humans. And if we accept the fact that they seem to be changing in their behavior, then perhaps the explanation is that they are evolving, just as you accept that the human has evolved. Why would this other being necessarily remain static in its nature or its function or its way of relating to us?"

Ambrose blurted a sound that sounded part chuckle, part sob. "It just occurred to me that if these 'others' are the powerful beings that we decided we would call gods, then you are suggesting that God is evolving!"

Sid smiled. "I'll leave it up to you to sort that out, but it does sound like something that you could put in your famous dictionary now that you are able to write again."

"Hmm . . . about that . . ." Ambrose growled pensively.

"What?" replied Sid. "What about that?"

"One might see that, too, as coming from these gods, my ability to write again. And if one were to examine the content of my missive on the day of Kiki's departure, one might suggest what I produced has something to do with moving from a state of disinterest to some sort of investment in the welfare of another."

"Caution, my man. Go too far with that and you might say you are being called to something beyond our current state."

Ambrose looked at Sid. "Why do I get the feeling that statement might be more about you than me? And why do I have this feeling of . . . apprehension?"

Sid smiled a beaming, glowing smile, a smile the strength of which had been fading in recent times but now returned as if he were lit from inside by a powerful star. "You are a very wise and perceptive one. I believe you know what I am getting ready to do."

Ambrose felt the sadness of many lifetimes of loss upon loss, and he could not bring himself to speak. He looked away and said only one word. "When?"

Sid answered softly, "I will be leaving. I will make this great crossing upon completion of my goodbye to you, my friend."

Ambrose's fear and sadness turned in an instant to rage. He considered dismissing Sid in anger and scorn, but he fought the fury. He gathered himself inside and did not reveal his true feeling. Sid remained silent until Ambrose spoke again.

"I held back when Kiki announced her departure, but I will give you this warning: You are taking a great risk. You know that you may be sent back here for another turn upon the earth, and if I understand Buddhism correctly, you may come back as a man or return here as a cockroach. Think about that, my great friend!"

Sid laughed. "Then the burden is on you. Whenever it is that you decide to cross and then return for another cycle upon the great blue and green orb—and that day will come—then you must take care with your soldier's boot to never squash another cockroach, because that bug may be your old friend."

Sharing smiles from one to the other, the two spirits kept quiet for a short measure of the earth's spin. Then Sid said to his friend, "I hope to return in some form that is midway between a six-legged citizen and a holy man. I think the life of a humble tailor or shoemaker in a small Mediterranean town would fit *my* true nature. I would welcome the ordinary struggle to please a wife and feed a child. I would welcome the burden of insufficient time to wrestle with cosmic truths."

"Then I hope you are right," said Ambrose. "I hope you are placed upon the string of whatever bow will shoot you back into a simple life, fat, burdened only by one too many children but with good company before the hearth—"

"There is one final question I have for you before I go." Sid paused, sensing quiet assent to pose his approaching query. "How did you die?"

Ambrose reacted with a barely perceptible smile. "I wondered why you never asked. I assumed you knew."

"We have noted many times that it is a puzzle why some things are known and some are not, but for some reason this is one of the things about you that I do not know. I did not observe your mortal demise. The story is neither preserved in human script or song nor carried on the wind. A puzzlement."

"Unlike your passing, a calamity of such proportions that it was preserved in hearts and minds worldwide?" A playful smile came with Ambrose's remark.

"Represented and misrepresented many times over," Sid returned.

Ambrose spoke with a chuckle. "The only notable fact about my passing is that I died having outlived all of my family and friends from the early part of my life. They took with them to their graves any memory of the time I was at my worst, when I was young and stupid, making the mistakes of my youth. Whether that serves one as advantage or not, it did give me the freedom to repeat those same stupid mistakes, and find new ones, in my later years without troublesome reminders. I dare say that we share that common experience."

Sid laughed and smiled back at Ambrose. "The witty and dark way you answer my question leads me to the obvious conclusion. You do not know how you died, do you? I dare say you were one of those fortunate people who perhaps died during sleep, your last waking thoughts reflecting neither triumph nor tragedy, but rather of nighttime ablutions and curiosity about the morning to come?"

"Let us just say that we must end this discussion with nothing that can be said positively, that is to say, *mistaken at the top of one's voice.*"[24]

With his final words, Sid turned away from Ambrose. He left slowly at first, walking away, not rising above ground, not floating in the air, but walking deliberately, purposefully, as if bound to the hard-packed dust of the planet. Ambrose watched each step as he grew smaller—a small, thin, bald Asian man in a tan robe. On he walked, growing ever smaller. And then he was gone. And despite having no watery tears to flow, Ambrose wept.

---

24 The definition of "positive" from *The Devil's Dictionary.*

CHAPTER 19

NEW BEGINNINGS

When Ambrose returned to Old Robin, all of those he called friends—some recent and others who endured over time—now gone. In the yard he noticed a sign that read SOLD placed over the previous offering of sale. Inside, downstairs, the house stood empty, save for the grand piano. He ascended the stairway toward the bedrooms and found them also empty except for the large mirror in which he and Kiki had noted their reflections upon first meeting.

He looked into the mirror. His own image stared back. He saw a weary if not broken man. Then, suddenly, words seemed to emerge above his reflection. He turned to look behind him to see if something was written on the wall and reflected in the mirror. Nothing. He turned back to the mirror and read the words.

Attend to your nature

Ambrose stood transfixed. He could not look away. His mind raced. He desperately wanted someone to talk to, even Victoria. Especially Victoria, whom he once dismissed as a person of little consequence but now held in esteem. Lost in thought, he then considered a new idea. Some things now seemed clear that once did not.

This house. This was where he first met Kiki, the new spirit who lost almost nothing of her concern for those living and those in the world of spirits. This was not supposed to be the way it was. Then Sid seemed to change. Did he start to change after Ambrose brought him here? It was from this house they were compelled to act to rescue Dave. No, it started for Sid before then. Didn't it?

Ambrose screamed, addressing it to himself. "This house! This damnable house! It's playing with my mind. Or something in it! I know it screamed when they ripped out the old stuff. They gutted it! Original and noble on the outside. Wounded and trying to heal on the inside. Forever changed! And now trying to change me! I curse the day I came here! I thought Kiki was giving me this house. Was it the other way around? Did the house give Kiki to me? For some purpose!"

Ambrose wandered, involuntarily, through the house, down the stairs, and through the kitchen, and out into the yard. His path was not his choice. He was not the guide of his journey. He calmed himself. He gave in to whom or what drove him. He moved upwards, high in the air, and looked down on the grand house, then surrendered to the force that pulled him away.

Driven along, not by the wind, but by intrusive thoughts and compelling instructions, Ambrose drew near to the wood now known regionally as the "haunted forest." A considerable measure of earthly time had passed since Sid's departure, and more time since Ambrose's last visit to the tall pines surrounding the open field of Dave's first grave site. For several years now, local teens and young adults had come to witness the unusual events in this forest, but their stays were always short. Some left terrified, others left in time to be merely amused by the sound that some heard as a growl, others described as a hiss, and others simply would not venture to name. No one yet claimed to have completed the dare of spending a full night camped in that place, despite the fact such a challenge was a popular one, sometimes taken up by boastful young people and attention seekers of all ages. Scores had come equipped with all manner of recording technology and even weaponry. Yet all who made the effort to stay had fled, humbled and terrified. No one had endured long enough to simply light a campfire. Few would even discuss what they had experienced.

On his way, Ambrose reflected on the last moments spent with his Buddhist companion. Sid had described to Ambrose his own journey to belief that it was time for him to return to the space of living, breathing, blood-pumping creatures, including humans, where Sid believed he was called to a purpose. Sid had confessed that he feared he would miss much of what he was going to leave behind. Foremost in his fears was the loss of his once complete attainment of peace and disinterest. He sadly reflected that such peace was no longer available to him in this spirit world.

Arriving at the location from which he had viewed the forest twice before, Ambrose felt relieved that the commands brought him here, to this location upon the spinning globe, and not toward a pathway for crossing over to the other side. He felt he was not ready to cross over. There were still things he wanted to do in the spirit world. He allowed himself to covet experiences and ideas about which he could write. The possibility he might be able to compose again filled him with an excitement that had been long missing from his current manifestation. He felt joyful. His thoughts drifted briefly away to an idea for a story about the haunted forest.

Ambrose then visited the memories of an earlier time, a time of youth and soldiering, *when all the world was beautiful and strange* to him. He reflected upon a time when *unfamiliar constellations burned in Southern midnights and the mockingbird pour out his heart from the moon-gilded Magnolia.* Distant memories placed *contrasting pictures athwart the harsher features of this later world accentuating the ugliness of the longer and tamer life.* The phantoms of a blood-stained era looked at him with tender eyes and smiled and gestured with airy grace. He reflected upon danger and horror, placing them beside the gracious and picturesque images of soldiering.[25]

Ambrose circled the haunted forest like a mounted scout, his heart in full ache for contact with the divine. Loss of mortal coil had no longer granted him transcendence of human care. He cried out to the wizard youth and asked for one more touch of the artist hand upon his troubled canvas, to gild for one more moment this present day. He offered a surrender of his present and of any prior or future life if only he could hold again, for just one moment the life of the warrior, the life he sought to throw away at Shiloh's battlefield.[26]

From deep within the haunted forest a growl broke the silence. Earthly winds shook real trees. Clouds formed instantaneously above and the sky grew dark. A hiss. Then another, turned to a growl. Ambrose felt uncertain. For just a moment he felt afraid, but soon his emotions turned in double measure to a peaceful and hopeful anticipation of . . . something. His mind became clear and focused. Unsure if he should credit his own self-affirmed wisdom or whether he was being taught at the knee of some unseen master, he became aware of the presence of a fractured spirit, and of his compassion for it and his own will to engage it. He moved closer to the woods. After a brief pause, he moved forward within the forest, and then above it, and passed over the vacant grave where Dave once lay.

The growl rose to a howl. The hiss became a great tearing and shaking. Lightning lit the sky and thunder expanded it. A

---

25 The above paragraph is a slightly altered representations of an appropriated narrative of Bierce's reflections taken from "What I Saw of Shiloh."

26 Ibid.

sense of motion gripped him and pulled him forward, toward . . . others. He willed himself to move slowly and with caution as if he were an actor upon a crowded stage.

Ambrose then felt something he knew he should not have felt. As spirit he had no skin, nor hair nor bone, indeed no corporeal form, but now he felt as if mortal capabilities were simulated if not restored. He reveled in a surge of energy moving through what form he did possess. He cried out in celebration, releasing one great scream of joy and of unspeakable pleasure, and he opened his spiritual arms to capture and enfold the broken spirit of the man who on the earth carried the name of Grover Wilson Ross.

EPILOGUE

By Ambrose Bierce

Thus concludes my account—or more accurately, I suppose I should say—Mr. Bridges's account of some of my experiences in the spirit world. Which part is literally true and which part is a manifestation of his creativity will remain unrevealed, as was our agreement when we formed our partnership. I trust we both will profit from our efforts. On balance, I am pleased.

You may, however, perceive me as lacking in gratitude in my next statement. Although I have now regained the ability to write, here in the spirit world, I do not credit Mr. Bridges for any measure of this. However, I am profoundly grateful to him for passing back to the mortal realm some of what I am now writing.

Those readers who are familiar with my work from a time when I drew breath and consorted with the earthbound will be familiar with my disdain for long pieces. I never understood that form of telling a story that came to be known as the "novel." It remains for me an indulgence of the highest order. In truth, this book required a partnership between the quick and the dead for me to tolerate a work of this length. I continue to be surprised that anyone should want to read or write such pieces.

As for the future, I will stay here and continue to write and pass on these efforts through my current living literary partner. How long I will do this, I am not sure. I will confess that the act of writing and my desire that it be found worthy of acclaim does not fire me as it once did. This is most likely the inevitable outcome of being here in the spirit world and I anticipate that someday I shall be more than ready to cross over to what awaits me on the other side.

In addition, I am, of course, aware that Mr. Bridges will eventually die and leave me without a mortal portal. Please note that I have promised him that I will stay here long enough to welcome him here and perhaps we will cross over together. I will discourage him from remaining here simply to see who reads his work. He will either forgive me for now saying, or at the very least he should understand that this is the kind of thing I might say, when I suggest that there may not be much continuing interest in his work after his departure from a world that is sadly turning a blind eye and deaf ear to the crafting of good stories.

I assume that you may be curious about the beings that I still can name only as "the others." I am entertaining a new idea that they are not divine beings. Indeed, they may be spirits who shared with us a common humanity but have now attained uncommon capabilities. In addition, I can't dismiss the idea that they have something fundamental to do with the house known as Old Robin.

Whatever their nature, they, of course, must be given credit for the communication I have had with Mr. Bridges, but beyond that, I have little to report. I continue to reside at Old Robin, and as far as I know have not disturbed the new owners. If the spirit of Mr. Bibby still resides here, he has not revealed himself.

Whatever is happening is proceeding slowly. Such is the nature of evolution, even as the world unfolds as it must. There has been virtually no communication from them, other than the fact that I receive occasional commands almost always when I am in the house. I seem to have been given a job to do. There are tortured souls caught between worlds. I have been chosen to reach out and open my arms to them. I accept this task on "faith" and in doing so I suppose I must revisit my infamous dictionary and alter, if not redefine, that troublesome word.[27]

In closing, I present to you in the Appendix of this work, my latest creation, sent from my current world to the land of the living.

---

27 The definition of "faith": "Belief without evidence in what is told by one who speaks without knowledge, of things without parallel." From *The Devil's Dictionary*.

THE PROFESSOR AND THE DEVIL

By Ambrose Bierce

I n the mid-twentieth century, a man made friends with the devil. His motivation to do so was honorable, since he was by profession a learned university teacher of history and religion. He correctly surmised that the devil would be a unique informant regarding matters of history that may be driven or colored by the religious beliefs of mortals. The two met monthly, in the professor's university café or some such place, for four decades.

The devil routinely took the physical form of a bearded, tweedy-looking companion who appeared to age at a rate matching that of the professor, thus attracting no attention from the larger body of learners who passed among them. In personal conversation the devil betrayed little emotion, presenting himself in a courteous if somewhat detached manner, but always eager to respond to the professor's inexhaustible curiosity about events that may have been influenced by the dark side of the spiritual cosmology.

Of course, the motivation of the devil to enter into this friendship was as one would expect: to steal a soul. He made no secret of the fact that he intended to find some vice, or coveted item, or enticing experience that would cause the professor to weaken and thus bargain away his eternity. So, as the two friends discussed war, sin, greed, and other notable human frailties and failures, the professor in full awareness and consent allowed the devil to tempt him. Temptation never won out, keeping the professor's soul out of harm's reach.

The professor often thanked his evil friend for his "dark but insightful perspective" and for sharing historical information available from no other source. The devil never gave the professor reason to doubt the truthfulness of this information, as it was not inconsistent with other historical sources.

On one occasion, the professor asked why the devil persisted in this friendship even after forty years of rejected enticements. The mortal man mused that the friendship clearly benefitted only himself. The devil replied that the relationship was hardly one-sided. On the contrary, answered the dark prince, the professor's remarkable resistance of all temptation had informed and strengthened the devil. In pursuit of others more open to temptation, the devil used this experience with the professor to overcome less resilient victims and drag them to hell. This information gave the professor some pause, but in the end, he concluded that the sum total of the friendship contributed to invaluable historical scholarship.

One day the professor revealed to the devil his sad news, "My friend, we will meet only a few more times. I have just come from my physician, and he tells me I have only months to live."

The devil replied, "Yes, I know that. Such things are always known to me before they are known to the soon-to-be departed." And after a brief pause, he added, "Oh, but please know this is not something I have brought about. I do not act in such a way in the mortal sphere; my only concern is the spirit . . . and I hope you know that even if I could so act—in the living world, that is—I would not bring that kind of harm to you, my friend."

In that brief moment, when the devil spoke of their friend-ship, the professor saw in the eyes of his companion something he had never seen before. He saw sadness, regret, and even empathy. They sat in comfortable silence for several minutes.

Then the devil spoke, "And it is clear you have won this test of will and character or whatever noble designation you wish to place upon your total resistance to my wickedness. I salute you and I wish to give you a gift."

The professor was wary, and at first refused the gift, but the devil continued, "And this is not about your soul. It is a gift you can accept or refuse, no equivalence of generosity is sought or will be accepted even if you offer."

"What sort of gift might benefit a dying man?" asked the professor.

In reply, the devil spoke without smile or any indication of pleasure that the professor showed interest, "I never told you that among my powers is the ability to travel through time, or more precisely to go backwards in time. I cannot and would not want to go forward in time, but that is another story. I will take you back in time to any historical event you choose and allow you to observe it, as if you were there when it occurred."

With this, the professor was intrigued. He pondered his choice only briefly, then spoke, "My mind is often drawn to an event that happened during the first of the world wars, often called the 'Christmas Truce,' when German and British soldiers put down their weapons and freely shared a moment of humanity despite the war that unfolded around them. Do you know of that day?"

"I do. I can take you there."

"Now?"

Putting down his napkin and taking a last sip of water, the devil replied, "Yes, this very moment, although I suggest we pay our bill and walk a bit beyond this place so that our sudden departure not be an event that calls attention to our journey."

Their business so transacted, the two walked side by side out of the café and turned the corner to witness such a scene that startled the professor sufficiently that he gave a gasp and muffled cry of surprise. Before them lay a field of battle, blue smoke lingering in the air, dimming the light of the late day sun. A few hundred paces in front of them, a tangle of wooden and metal impediments connected by barbed wire stretched out menacingly in order to guard an elaborate network of trenches.

They turned to look behind them and saw a similar construction, but being closer to this second grouping, could see men relaxing, some sleeping within their embattlements. In the open space between the two armies, men from each side stood in groups of twos, threes, and tens, talking and smiling. Further down the lines, the sound of music gave background; the two companions paused to listen to the singing of Christmas carols, voices alternately German, then English, but lifting the same songs up to a smiling, common heaven.

The two friends walked closer to the soldiers and saw two men, one a German, the other British, take scissors and remove buttons from their uniforms to trade with the other. Combatants from both sides displayed pictures of wives and girlfriends and children to their foe, the lack of a common language no barrier to mutual appreciation of the joys that awaited their homecoming when war was done. A short distance away, warrior enemies set their weapons aside and became athletes, kicking a ball in an impromptu game of football.

The devil spoke in response to a smile from the professor, "Is this what you came to see?"

The professor's smile grew wider and he looked the devil in

the face and said, "This is what I wanted you to see. I wanted you to see, before our time together ended, evidence of man's essential goodness. These men, not one of them, is by nature evil, notwithstanding the killing done. I offer it as prologue to your own ultimate demise, my friend. You will not win the day as long as hearts such as these beat in human chests. Perhaps that is why you fear the future."

The two stood in contemplation of each other without words. Then the professor spoke, "I am done here. We can go home now."

"What do you mean?" replied the devil.

"Back to our world, beside the café."

The devil then spoke without emotion, on his face a cold, lifeless gaze. "Oh no. I promised that I would bring you here. I said nothing about taking you back. You are now here to stay. I will be going now. But you will not. I suggest you get back to your trench and get some sleep, tomorrow the guns will again cry out and you are in for a very difficult day. You may want to reflect upon the meaning of hubris, or whatever you wish to name as your own failing."

APPROPRIATIONS

Phrases and descriptions used previously by Ambrose Bierce in his own writing have been appropriated for use here in the service of storytelling. When the appropriations are exact quotes, the words are italicized. Other appropriations are paraphrased representations of the original work.

REFERENCES

The phrases and descriptions, the "appropriations," that appear in this book were taken from the following source:

Bierce, Ambrose. *The Devil's Dictionary, Tales & Memoirs*, edited by S.T. Joshi. New York: Library of America 2011.

To read other works by Ambrose Bierce, visit http://www.ambrosebierce.org/works.html.

ACKNOWLEDGEMENTS

T hank you to my writing group: Gale, Christy, Lauren. Robin and Michael for guidance at the very first days of this writing. Thank you to Bill Finger for his insights as the work evolved.

I am grateful to Terri Leidich, President and Publisher of BQB Publishing, for believing that this book belonged on the shelf beside the works of the other remarkable writers at BQB.

Most of all, I owe a debt to Caleb Guard for his edits both developmental and otherwise. I'm sure he will embrace Ambrose Bierce's definition of "editor" from *The Devil's Dictionary*.

EDITOR, n. A person who combines the judicial functions of Minos, Rhadamanthus and Aeacus but is placable with an obolus; a severely virtuous censor . . . Master of mysteries and lord of law, high-pinnacled upon the throne of thought, his face suffused with the dim splendors of Transfiguration, his legs intertwisted and his tongue a-cheek, the editor spills his will along the paper and cuts it off in lengths to suit.

ABOUT THE AUTHOR

Drew Bridges is a retired psychiatrist who has restored himself to his default identity of English major. His restoration included operating a bookstore for seven years in the town of Wake Forest, NC, where he lives with his wife, Lauren, a psychotherapist.

He has published five previous books that cover a broad range of topics including a previous novel, memoir, sports, and some featuring psychological themes.

OTHER BOOKS
BY DREW BRIDGES
THAT ARE PUBLISHED BY BQB PUBLISHING

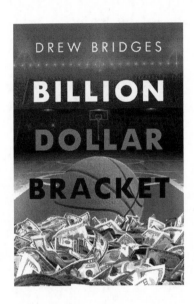

Many lives collide in this quest to win a billion dollars for picking all the winners in the annual National Collegiate Athletic Association basketball tournament. Some are looking for riches, others for simple survival and personal redemption.

Mathematician Sinclair Dane sponsors the contest, seeking money for a safety net for her troubled mother. She does not have a billion dollars to pay a winner. Risking her reputation and possible legal charges for fraud, she pins her hopes on the astronomical odds against anyone picking all the winners.

Math professor Lewis Cusac uses the basketball contest to teach remedial math to college students, two of whom are playing in the tournament. He enters the contest and finds himself having selected all the winners with only three games remaining. He also gets a call from the NCAA investigators for suspicion of trying to fix the outcomes of games.

Add to the mix a retired casino operator, a group of twenty-something social media wizards, and professional basketball's next megastar. As the contest goes global, the story races to an ending that will surprise the reader.